・我認為小王子的出走，必定是借助移棲的侯鳥群之力。

有人說《小王子》不只是青少年的經典，它也是成人的童話。
自一九四三年出版以來，一直是全世界讀者的最愛、
《小王子》也是繼《聖經》之後，全世界最暢銷的、最歷久彌新的書。

The Little Prince

中英文彩色版

聖·修伯里〔著〕
楊玉娘〔譯〕

1

　　六歲那年，我曾在某部書裏看到一幀頗為壯觀的圖畫，描繪的是原始森林裏的景象，名喚「大自然的真相」。畫中有條大蟒蛇正在吞噬一隻野獸；此即為原圖之影本。

　　書上說：「蟒蛇嚼都不嚼，一口將整隻獵物吞到肚子裏，因而動彈不得。此後，為了消化這頓大餐，牠整整休眠了六個月之久。」

　　看過這段圖文，我陷於深沈的遐思中，擬想那叢林野地裏的種種奇遇。然後手執彩筆，畫下第一張圖畫。我的第一幅畫如下：

我把這幅傑作捧到大人們面前，問他們這幅畫有沒有把他們給嚇到了？

他們卻答道：「嚇到？誰會被一頂帽子給嚇到啊？」

我畫的才不是帽子呢！那是蟒蛇吞象後消化時的模樣呀！不過，既然大人們都看不懂，我就另外畫一張好了；於是我畫出蟒蛇腹中的蠕動情形。這樣一來，大人們就可以一眼瞧得明明白啦！他們什麼事都得要人解釋得一清二楚才成。我的第二幅畫如下：

這次大人們的反應是：要我別管什麼外觀圖、內在圖，全扔到一旁去，專心唸唸地理、歷史、算術和文法才是正經事。正因如此，我在六歲時便放棄了可能成為畫家的這個偉大夢想。第一、二幅畫的失敗，早已使我沮喪萬分。大人們從不主動去理解任何事，而對孩子們來說，成天向他們解釋這、解釋那的，有多煩人哪！因此，我選擇了另一行：學習駕駛飛機。我大抵飛過世界各地；地理對我而言，還真管用呢！只要隨意一瞄，我便能分辨出某地是中國或亞利桑那。若有人夜間迷途的話，這點知識就夠寶貴的了。

這段里程中，我接觸到許許多多日後舉足輕重的人物。我和大人們共同生活，關係密切，並仔細觀察他們。但這並未增進我對他們的觀感。

每當我碰到某個自己看來覺得有賞析能力的人，便嘗試著把一直隨身攜帶的第一幅畫拿給他看，藉此我便可以測出對方是否真的很有頭腦。

然而，無論是男人、女人，全都信誓旦旦地說：

「那是頂帽子。」

如此一來，我將不再同這個人談論蟒蛇、原始森林或星星之類的事了。我會降低水準配合他，說些橋啊、高爾夫啊、政治或領帶等等的話題，而那個大人也會為了碰到這麼聰敏的人而大感興奮哩！

2

直到八年前在撒哈拉沙漠出了點意外為止，我一直沒能碰到那個真正談得來的人，所以一直過得很孤獨。那天，我的引擎故障，身邊又沒有任何技師或乘客，只得一個人努力嘗試修好機器。當時我能否活得下去還大有問題，因為身邊帶的飲用水，勉強只夠撐上一個禮拜。

於是，第一天夜晚，我就在杳無人跡的荒漠中睡著了。當時的處境比遇上船難、在汪洋中乘著小筏東漂西蕩的水手還孤立無依哩！所以嘍！您應可以想像得到，當翌晨旭日初昇，我突然被一個微弱而奇特的聲音喚醒時，內心有多驚訝！那聲音說：

「拜託你——幫我畫隻綿羊！」

「什麼？！」

「幫我畫隻綿羊！」

我目瞪口呆地跳了起來，驚訝得猛眨眼，仔細地搜尋四周。然後看到一名小得異常的小人兒，站在那兒、鄭重地凝視著我。底下便是我後來竭盡所能，以他為藍本畫下的素描。當然，我的畫遠不及他本人那樣迷人啦！

不過呢，這可不是我的錯。遠在我才六歲時，大人們就已使我成為畫家的志向為之一挫。而除了蟒蛇吞象的外觀圖、內在圖外，我就再也不曾嘗試畫過任何東西了。

我瞪大雙眼、訝異地凝視著眼前這條忽而來的詭異人物——記著！我可是置身於杳無人煙的大沙漠呵！然而，這小人兒看起來一點也不像在沙漠中迷了路，也全沒因飢渴、疲乏或恐懼而虛脫的模樣；渾身上下，瞧不出一絲在荒漠中迷途的那種孩童的跡象。最後，我終於鎮定些了，這才開口問他：

　　「你——你在這裏做什麼呀?!」

　　他以異常緩慢的聲調重申那句話，彷彿訴說某件非比尋常的大事似的：

　　「拜託您——幫我畫隻綿羊……」

　　每當事情透著強烈的神祕氣氛時，人們總是無力抗拒。儘管置身於無人的曠野，面臨死亡威脅時，畫畫對我來說簡直荒唐透頂，我還是從口袋裏掏出紙和自來水筆來。然而，這時我猛地想起，過去我一直被迫專注於地理、歷史、算術、文法。於是，我告訴那小傢伙（並且是個小頑固）說我不曉得該怎麼畫。他回答我說：「沒有關係，畫隻綿羊給我……」

可是我從沒畫過綿羊呀！於是我為他畫了自己最常畫的那兩個圖案中的一個，也就是蟒蛇吞象的外觀圖。可是，那小傢伙對它的評判卻教我嚇一大跳，他說：

「不，不，不！我不要巨蟒吞象。大蟒蛇這生物十分危險，而大象也太笨重了。在我居住的地方，每樣東西都非常小。我要的是隻綿羊，請幫我畫隻綿羊吧！」

於是我畫了一張圖。

他仔細的端詳一番，然後說：

「不，這隻綿羊好憔悴，再幫我畫一張吧！」

因此我又另畫了一張。

我的朋友無可奈何般溫和地微微一笑。

「你自個兒瞧瞧，」他說：「那不是綿羊，是牡羊，牠長角了。」

所以啊，我只好再畫一幅嘍！

可是他的反應還是一樣：

「這隻太老啦！我要一隻能活好久的綿羊。」

這下子我的耐性全被磨光了，我趕著修好引擎離開這地方，是以潦潦草草揮就這張圖。隨口扯個解釋：

「這只是牠的箱子；你要的綿羊

在裏頭。」

眼見這少年評審的臉上浮現一抹歡欣，我反倒驚異莫名，他表示：

「我就是要這個樣子呀！你認為這隻綿羊牠需不需要吃很多的草呢？」

「為什麼？」

「因為我住的地方，什麼東西都好小……」

「牠絕對有足夠的草吃。」我說：「我給你的這隻羊也很小哇！」

他低下頭去看那幅畫：

「沒那麼小——看，牠睡著了！」

這就是我結識小王子的經過。

我花了好長一段時間，才搞清楚小王子是打哪兒來的，因為他問了我好多問題，對我的問話卻置若罔聞一般。漸漸地，我才從他偶然吐露的點點滴滴間，明瞭所有的事情。

比如：他第一次看到我的飛機時（我不畫飛機了；畫它對我而言太複雜了些）問我：

「那是什麼東西啊？」

「那不是東西，它會飛，是一架飛機；我的飛機。」

告訴他我能飛這回事令我十分驕傲。

他一聽尖叫了起來：

「什麼！你是從天上掉下來的？」

「是的。」我鄭重地回答著。

「喔！真有意思！」

小王子爆出一串悅耳的笑聲，卻惹得我相當著惱；我希望別人能認真地看待我的不幸遭遇。

　　接著他又說：

　　「這麼說你也是從天上來的嘍！你來自哪個星球呢？」

　　就在這一刻，我對他那無從探索的神祕身世抓住了一線曙光，於是我斷然地追究道：

　　「你是從別的星球來的嗎？」

　　他卻不答話，只是專注地盯著我的飛機看，略略點個頭，說：

　　「就憑這東西，你確實不可能來自非常遙遠的地方……」

　　而後他便陷入沉思中。經過好一段時間，他又從口袋裏掏出我畫給他的綿羊，埋首審視他的寶藏。

　　您應可以想像得到，這半信半疑的「另一個星球」的問題，勾起我多大的好奇心。因此，我很努力的在這個話題中發掘更多的真相。

　　「小小人兒，你是從哪裏來的呢？你所謂『我住的地方』叫什麼？你要把你的綿羊帶到哪裏去呢？」

他先是默默沈思一陣，才回答道：

「你給我那盒子真是太棒了！這一來，到了夜晚，那盒子便可以當牠休息的房子了。」

「沒錯。而且，如果你循規蹈矩的話，我還會給你一條繩子，讓你在白天時把牠綁起來；還可以給你一根柱子，給你繫繩子用。」

然而，小王子卻似乎被這個建議給嚇著了：「把牠綁起來！多奇怪的念頭哇！」

「可是，如果你不把牠綁起來，」我說：「牠會到處亂逛，然後走丟了嘜！」

我的朋友又爆出另一串銀鈴似的笑聲：「你認為牠會逛到哪裏去呢？」

「任何地方都可能呀！直往前走就是了。」

這時，小王子誠摯地說：

「沒有關係，在我住的地方，一切都是很小的。」

他隱約帶點傷感地加上一句：

「就讓牠直往前走吧！沒有人能夠走太遠的……」

藉此，我又了解到第二個重要的事實：小王子所居住的星球，恐怕不見得比一幢房屋還大。

不過，這個事實倒沒令我特別吃驚。我清楚得很，宇宙中除了一些我們已命名的巨型星球如地球、木星、火星、金星外，還有許多數不清的星體；其中有的甚至小得用望遠鏡都很難觀測得到。天文學家發現這種小星星時，通常只是為它編個號碼，而不幫它命名：好比稱它為「小行星325」，之類的。

・（B-612 小行星上的小王子）

我認為小王子必定是來自那個叫作B-612的小行星。這顆小行星僅在一九〇九年時，由一名土耳其天文學家透過望遠鏡看到過一次而已！

　　此天文學家曾將他的發現呈報國際天文協會，以茲證明。然而，由於當時他穿的是土耳其服裝，以致沒有人肯相信他的話。

　　大人就是這樣……

　　幸而當時有位著名的土耳其獨裁者頒布一道命令，命其子民改著歐洲式服裝，違者處死；這才使得小行星B-612之名得以保存下來。一九二〇年，那名科學家身著高雅服裝，風度翩翩地重新提出報告；這次每個人都接受了。

　　我之所以涓滴不漏地細述有關這顆小行星的事，並一再提及它的編號，只為了那些大人們和他們的瑩性而已。大人們喜歡數字。當你告訴他們你交了個新朋友時，他們絕不會問你任何屬於本質上的問題。他們不會問：「他的聲音聽起來怎麼樣？他最喜歡玩什麼遊戲？他採集蝴蝶嗎？」而是問：「他幾歲？有幾個兄弟？幾公斤重？父親每個月的收入有多少？」惟有如此，他們才肯相信自己完全了解他。

　　要是你跟大人們說：「我看見一幢漂亮的紅甄屋，窗口攀繞天竺葵，簷前鴿子繞樑飛。」他們根本想像不出那房屋是什麼模樣。你應當這樣講：「我看到一幢值兩萬法郎的房子。」他們才會大呼：「哇！多美麗的房子呀！」

以此類推，你或許會告訴他們：「的確有小王子這個人存在。他又可愛、又會笑，他在找尋一隻綿羊；既然有人想找一隻綿羊，他必然是存在的。」但這些話有什麼用呢？他們必會聳聳肩，認為你還太小。不過，如果你跟他們說：「他來自B-612號小行星。」他們便不會再有疑問，而完全相信你的話了。

大人都是這樣，誰也無法改變這種習性！而孩子們則只好一直對他們百般忍耐了。

不過，對於我們這些了解生命的人而言，數目字顯然無關緊要。我原想以神話形式著手寫這個故事，告訴大家：「從前有個小王子，他住在一顆比他個頭大不了多少的星球上，他想要一隻羊……」

對於了解生命的人而言，這樣的故事真實多了。

因為，我可不願意任何人在閱讀我這本書時，只是草率的瀏覽一番而已。記下這些往事，已經教我很難受了。自我的朋友帶著他的羊離我而去，至今已有六年了。我之所以要試著詳細描述他，只怕自己日後忘了他，忘記朋友是件很悲哀的事；並非每個人都有朋友的。而且，倘若我忘了他的話，很可能就會變得像那些除了數字以外，對什麼都漠不關心的人一樣……

　　為了這個緣故，我又去買了盒顏料和一些鉛筆。人到了這個年紀，再要重拾畫筆委實不易；何況我自六歲時畫過蟒蛇吞象圖後，就再也不曾畫過任何一張圖了。我盡可能把畫畫得逼真生動，能否成功就沒把握了。這一幅或許進行得很不錯，那一幅卻又畫得離了譜。我還犯了些錯誤，就像小王子的身高部分：有時畫得高駝、有時畫得矮小；而他服裝的顏色我也不太確定。所以我只能盡力而為，畫得時好時壞，希望大致上還看得過去才好。

　　也許還有些重要的細節我沒弄對，不過這可不能怪我；我的朋友從沒向我解說些什麼。或許，他認為我和他沒什麼兩樣吧！而事實上，我卻連怎樣透視盒子四壁，看到裏面那隻小綿羊都不知道呢！或許我已經有點像大人了，我畢竟不小嘍！

　　日子一天天的過去，每天我都可以經由和小王子的交談，多知道一些有關他的星球、他的別離，以及他的旅程方面的事。這些資料，都是經由他沈思時不經意間吐露的話，一點一滴慢慢累積而成的。就在這種情況下，我在第三天時聽到木棉樹所引起的大災禍。

　　這次，我仍得感謝那隻綿羊。因為小王子突然問我 —— 彷彿十分擔憂地 ——「真的?!那隻綿羊真的只吃矮小的灌木嗎？」

　　「當然是真的呀！」

　　「啊！我真高興！」

我不明白為何那隻綿羊是否只吃灌木會有這麼重要。不過，小王子接下去又說：

　　「還有個問題：牠們也吃木棉嗎？」

　　我提示小王子，木棉不是灌木；相反的木棉樹能長到像城堡一般高大，甚至如果他趕著一群大象來吃的話，還吃不了一棵大木棉樹哩！

　　趕象群的主意逗得小王子哈哈大笑，他說：

　　「那咱們可得讓這群大象疊羅漢才成。」

　　不過，他也做了個很聰明的討論：

　　「在木棉樹還沒長到那麼高大以前，最初也是很小的。」

　　「這話對極啦！」找說：「可是，你為什麼想要綿羊去吃小木棉呢？」

　　他立刻大呼：「哦！得了！得了！」彷彿他所說的事是理所當然似的；所以，我只好獨自努力來解開這個謎團了。

　　事實上，據我所知，在小王子居住的星球上──正如所有的星球上一般──有好植物和壞植物之分。自然，好植物結好種子，壞植物則結壞種子。然而，這些種子一直長眠於幽黯的地底下，大家都看不見，直到其中某一顆忽然醒來，這才萌芽滋長，並開始──最初只是怯怯地──迎向陽光、舒展討人喜愛的嫩枝。假使那只是蘿蔔或玫瑰的小枝芽，人們便會任它自由自在、隨意生長。但若那是棵壞植物，人們便會在剛認山來時，立刻毀了它。

　　在小王子所居住的星球上，也有好些可怕的壞種子；那就是木棉子。星體上的土壤飽受木棉子蹂躪，若太晚發現其樹苗的話，就再也無法根除盡淨了。它的根會到處蔓延，盤據整個星球。萬一這顆星體太小，而木棉樹太多的話，這些樹便會將整個星球搞得四分五裂⋯⋯

　　「這是訓練問題。」小王子後來告訴我：「每天一早梳洗過後，就必須認認真真、仔仔細細地清理自己的星球。木棉剛長幼苗時，和玫瑰欉看來十分相似，因此得小心分辨出來，一旦發現，就要立刻拔得乾乾淨淨。這種工作枯燥又乏味，」小王子又追加一句：「但也非常容易。」

　　有一天，他對我說：「你應該畫幅漂亮的畫。這樣，你故鄉的孩子就可以知悉一切了。萬一哪天他們想旅遊的話，那畫就很派得上用場了！」他又說：「有時候，把某件事拖到第二天再做不會有什麼大礙。不過，若是事關木棉的話，拖一天很可能就會釀成大禍了。我知道一個住著個懶人的星球，他因疏忽三棵小樹

・木棉樹

苗，便……」

於是，我根據小王子的描述，畫下那個星球的情形。我並不喜歡以諄諄教誨的口氣說話，但是人們對於木棉的危險性幾乎一無所知，而此等重大危機又是任何在小行星迷途的人都可能造成的，是以我不只一次打破沈默，明白告誡：「孩子們，當心木棉樹！」我的朋友都和我一樣，長期瀕臨此種危機卻一無所覺；因此，為了他們，我必須好好下功夫畫這幅圖畫。如此費心費力做這件事，若能使大夥兒有所領悟，便值回一切了。

或許你會問我：「為何這本書裏所有的插畫，沒有一張像這幅那麼壯觀、深刻的？」

答案很簡單，我努力過，但畫別張圖時卻總不成功，而畫這幅木棉圖時，我卻為某種迫切需要的力量所激勵，而超越了自身的水準。

哦！小王子！我一點一滴地了解你那悲傷小生命中的祕密……好一陣子，唯一令你感興趣的娛樂，便是觀賞日落那份寧靜的樂趣。我是在第四天早上，才知道這段新情節的。當時你對我說：

「我好喜歡落日。走，現在讓我們一起去看夕陽吧！」

「可是我們得等等呀！」我說。

「等？等什麼？」

「等太陽下山啊！我們必須等到黃昏時候才行。」

最初你似乎驚訝萬分，後來又自嘲地笑笑，告訴我：

「我老當自己還在家裏呢！」

就是這個道理，每個人都曉得，美國正午時分，恰是法國日落之時。如果你能在一分鐘內飛抵法國，就可以從日正當中直接跳到日落。只可惜，一分鐘飛到法國根本辦不到。但是，親愛的小王子，在你的小星球上，無論什麼時候，只要你高興，把座椅移個幾步，便可以觀賞落日黃昏……

「有一天，」你跟我說：「我看了四十四次日落。」

稍停一歇，你又說：

「你曉得的，當一個人悲傷時，總是喜歡看夕陽。」

「這麼說，你看了四十四次日落那天，」我問道：「是很傷心的嘍？」

然而，小王子並沒有回答。

7

　　第五天——跟往常一樣，我又得感謝那隻綿羊——小王子再度洩露出他生命中的祕密。這個問題大概已經在腦海裏盤據好久了，他突如其來地探問：

　　「綿羊——如果綿羊吃小灌木的話，是不是也會吃花呢？」

　　「綿羊嘛——」我回答：「綿羊是找到什麼吃什麼的。」

　　「連帶刺的花也吃嗎？」

　　「是的，就算帶刺的花牠也吃。」

　　「那麼——長那些刺有什麼用呢？」

　　「我不知道。」那時我正忙著想弄鬆一顆卡在引擎上的螺絲釘，心裏很煩。因為，這時我已經察覺，飛機受損的情形顯然十分嚴重。而更令我心慌的是，身邊的飲用水已經所剩無幾了。

　　「那些刺——有什麼用呢？」

　　小王子再度追問；他是那種一有疑問絕不善罷干休的人。而我呢？我正為那顆螺絲釘焦躁不已，於是毫不思索地回答他說：

　　「那些刺一點用處也沒有；花長刺只為害人而已！」

　　「哦！」

　　沈寂了好一段時間，小王子突然憤慨地反駁我：

　　「我不信！花兒是很脆弱的生物，她們天真無邪，盡可能自我保護。她們相信那些刺是很厲害的武器、足以自衛……」

　　我沒回答。那時我正喃喃自語：「要是螺絲釘還不轉動，我就用榔頭把它敲下來。」小王子再度打斷我的思緒：

　　「你真的認為那些花的……」

　　「哦！不！」我大叫：「不！不！不！我什麼也不認為。我根本就是不假思索地回答。你難道沒看到我正忙著要緊的事嗎？」

他震驚地凝視著我。

「要緊的事？」

他看著我；我手上拿著榔頭，手指被機油弄得黑漆漆的，彎著身子在察看某樣他似乎覺得很醜的東西……

「你的語氣就和那些大人一樣！」

我一聽有點慚愧，可是他還是毫不容情的指責下去：

「你把每件事都搞混了……你把每件事都扯在一起……」

他真的非常生氣，用力地猛搖頭，金黃的捲髮在風中飄來盪去。

「我知道在某個星球上，住著一名紅臉紳士。他從沒嗅過任何一朵花，也沒注視過哪顆星星或愛過任何人。一生中除了把一些數字加起來外，從沒做過任何事。他整天唸來唸去只有一句話，就是你說的那句：『我正忙著要緊的事！』這可使他愈來愈高傲了。不過，他不算是人——他是個毒蕈！」

「是個什麼？」

「是個毒蕈！」

小王子氣得滿臉煞白。

「數百萬年來，花兒身上一直長著刺。而數百萬年來，綿羊也依舊吃花。難道試著了解花兒為何要那麼費勁地長些沒用的刺，這事就不要緊嗎？綿羊和花兒之間的爭端也不要緊嗎？這些都沒紅臉紳士的數字重要嗎？如果我——我本人

——認識一朵長在我星球上的稀世奇葩，他卻可能在某天早上，被一隻小羊糊塗地一口咬掉——天啊！你竟認為這事不打緊！」

他接著說下去；臉色由白轉紅：

「天上星辰難以計數。但若是其中一顆星上長著某人深愛的一朵花；那麼，即使只是遙望那些星星，他也會快樂無比。他可以對自己說：『在某個地方，我的花兒……』然而，如果綿羊把花吃掉了，那他眼中的星星都會霎時黯淡無光了……而你竟認為這不重要！」

他抽抽咽咽，再也說不出話來。暮色低垂，我將手中的工具全扔掉；在這一刻，我的榔頭、我的螺絲釘，或者飢渴、死亡算什麼呢？在一顆星星，一個星體——我的星體——地球上，有個小王子需要人安慰。我摟著他，輕搖著他說：

「你深愛的那朵花不會有危險的。我會幫你的綿羊畫個口罩，再畫個柵欄給你放在那朵花旁，我會……」

我不知道該對他說些什麼。只覺得自己好笨，犯了個大錯。我不知道怎麼才能接近他、感動他，彼此重新再度攜手。

淚之鄉是個多麼神祕的地方呵！

沒多久，我對這朵花便有了更深一層的認識。在小王子居住的星球上，花兒通常都很單純。它們只有一圈花瓣，既不佔空間，又不會騷擾到任何人。某天早上，它們開放在草地上；到了夜晚，便又靜靜地消失。然而有一天，不知從哪個地方吹來一顆種子，開始生長。小王子小心翼翼地觀察這株和星球上其他花苗都不相像的嫩芽，說不定這是另一種和木棉相似的植物哩！

不過，這棵植物很快便不再向上長，並開始抽出花苞。小王子一眼看到那個大花苞，心中就覺得裏頭似乎隱藏著某種古靈精怪的東西。但這朵花對自己降落在這一片翠綠的落腳處，來準備綻放美麗的容顏感到非常不滿。她戒慎萬端地選擇自己的顏色、慢吞吞地打扮、一一打點自己的花瓣。她可不想和遍地的罌粟花一般，皺巴巴地來到這世界！她希望自己一現身，就是光芒四射、美麗耀眼。喔！是呀！她的確是風情萬種的！而她那神奇的裝扮工作一直持續了好幾天。

後來有天早上，正當旭日東昇時，她忽然綻放嬌顏了。

歷經所有備嘗艱辛的預備工作後，她打了個呵欠說：

「唉！我還沒完全清醒過來呢！請你千萬原諒，我的花瓣還亂糟糟……」

可是，小王子已經忍不住要讚美：

「哇！妳太漂亮了！」

「可不是嗎？」那朵花嬌滴滴地回答：「我是在陽光昇起時誕生的哪……」

小王子可以輕輕鬆鬆地斷定，她一點兒也不謙虛——然而，她是多麼動人、多麼有朝氣呀！

「我想該是早餐時間了，」沒多久她又說：「拜託你給我些……」

小王子一聽，忸怩不安，跑開去找了一壺清新的水來。從此，他開始照顧這朵花。

而她呢？由於虛榮心的作祟，也很快為他惹來麻煩——要是他早知如此，就不可能這麼好商量了。比方說，有一天她提到身上的四個刺時，便告訴小王子：

「老虎要來張牙舞爪就讓牠們來吧，我可不怕！」

「我的星球上沒有老虎，」小王子不同意她的話：「再說，老虎根本不吃雜草。」

「我才不是雜草呢！」那花兒愛嬌地說：

「對不起，我……」

「我一點都不怕老虎，」她接下去說：「不過，我好怕刮風哦！我猜，你大概沒幫我準備屏風吧？」

「怕風──對植物而言，那真是不太好哩！」小王子說完這話，又自言自語道：「這朵花可真不單純……」

「晚上，我希望你能幫我弄個玻璃罩；你這地方可真冷呵！在我家鄉……」

她說到這裏，猛然自行住口。她來的時候還不過是顆種子，對其他的世界根本一無所知。她怕這無知的謊言被拆穿，窘得咳了兩三聲，好轉移小王子的注意力。

「屏風呢？」

「妳剛說話時，我正想去找一個來……」

她勉強自己再咳幾聲，免得他後悔了。

因此，小王子雖然出於愛護她而殷殷照料，卻很快就不肯輕易相信她了。常常，他聽起來好像很要緊的事，事實上卻是無關緊要，這使得他非常不高興。

「我當初真不該聽她的。」有天他跟我表白：「人不該聽花的話，只要欣賞她們、聞聞她們的芳香就好了。我那朵花使整個星球瀰漫著香氣，我卻無法從中得到樂趣。關於老虎爪那篇鬼話；我應該只要滿心憐憫和關愛就夠了！」

他直言無諱：

「老實說，我完全不懂該如何了解任何一件事！我應該依據行為，而不是依據談話去下判斷才對。她對我飄送芳香、綻放光彩，我不該離她而去……我早該想到隱藏在她那些可憐兮兮的小把戲下有著深刻的感情。花兒總是很矛盾的！可是那時我太年輕，不知道該怎樣去愛她……」

我相信小王子出走時，必定是借助移棲的野鳥群之助。在離開故鄉那天早上，他一絲不苟地處理好小行星上的各項事物，並細心地清理自己的火山。他有兩座活火山，正好可以供他熱早餐用；此外還有一座死火山。不過，正如他所說的：「天知道以後會出什麼事！」是以他連那座死火山也清理乾淨了。火山一旦清理妥當後，便會穩定而沈穩地燃燒，而不會突然爆發。火山一爆發，就好像煙囪裏的烈焰般。

相形之下，地球上的人類和火山一比，就顯得太渺小了，小得無力清理火山。正因如此，火山才會帶給我們人類無窮無盡的困擾。

小王子又垂頭喪氣地拔除最後那幾棵小木棉樹苗；他相信自己是不可能再回來了。然而，在這最後一個早上，平日熟悉的工作似乎都顯得無比珍貴了。就在他最後一次為花兒澆水，準備幫她蓋好玻璃罩時，真覺得自己快掉下眼淚了。

「再見！」他對那朵花兒說。

花兒卻沒回答。

「再見！」他再說一遍。

‧小王子細心地清理他的活火山

花兒咳嗽了；不過，可不是因為冷。

「我以前真傻，」最後，她告訴他：「求你原諒我！試著快樂些……」

她竟沒有責罵他，讓他感到十分驚訝。他丈二金剛摸不著頭腦，愣愣地站在那兒，手中的玻璃罩揚在半空中；這一番的溫文甜蜜，反倒教他茫然不解。

「我當然愛你！」花兒告訴他：「一直沒能讓你明瞭，那是我的錯。這並不重要；可是你 —— 你一直就跟我一樣笨。快樂些吧！把玻璃罩扔掉，我再也不需要它了。」

「可是風會 ——」

「冷對於我並不是真的那麼糟……我是一朵花，夜晚的涼風對我有益。」

「可是那些動物會 ——」

「喂！如果我有心結交蝴蝶的話，總得忍受兩三條毛毛蟲嘛！那些蝴蝶看起來真漂亮。而且，除了蝴蝶和毛毛蟲外，還有誰會來拜訪我呢？你就要遠走……至於那些大動物 —— 我才不怕牠們呢！喏！我有爪子。」她天真地展示身上那四個刺，又說：

「別這麼遲疑了，你都下決心要走了，現在就走吧！」

因為，她不想讓小王子看到自己在哭泣；她是一朵如此驕傲的花……

10

他發現小行星325，326，327，328，329和330跟自己的星球相鄰，便開始逐一拜訪它們，好教自己長點見識。

第一顆星星上住著一位國王。他身穿皇家紫貂袍，坐在一把樣式簡單而高貴的龍椅上。

「哇！有個子民來了！」他一看到小王子來到便立刻尖叫。

小王子自問：

「他從沒見過我，怎麼會認得我呢？」

他不了解在每個國王心目中，世界都是很單純的；他們把每個人都當成是自己的子民。王者說：「靠近一點，讓我好好看你。」

小王子四下張望，想找個地方坐下來。可是，整個星球都被國王那件華麗的貂袍給擠滿了，他只好還是直板板地站著。不過，他實在困倦極了，便打了個呵欠！

「在國王面前打呵欠不太像話了，」那王者對他說：「不許這樣！」

「我沒辦法；忍不住啊！」小王子好窘：「我剛奔波過好長一段路，到現在都還沒睡……」

「喔！那麼，」國王說：「我命令你打呵欠。我有好幾年沒見過人打呵欠了，打呵欠在我眼中倒是件挺稀奇的事。快！快！趕緊再打呵欠！這是命令。」

「這太嚇人了……我沒……沒辦法再打……」小王子慌得不得了，講起話來吞吞吐吐的。

「嗯！嗯！」國王答覆：「那麼，我命令你時而打呵欠，時而……」

他好像有點焦急，講得口沫橫飛的。

因為，別人必須尊重他的權威，這是身為國王最基本的堅持。他無法忍受反抗；他是個絕絕對對的統治者。不，因為他是個老好人，所以下的命令也都十分合理。

「如果我命令一名將軍，」他舉了個例子說：「如果我命令一名將軍變成海軍，那名將軍卻不服從我的命令，那麼，錯不在他而在我。」

「我可以坐下來嗎？」小王子怯怯地提出要求。

「我命令你坐下！」國王回答，並高貴地將自己的貂袍摺了幾摺。

可是小王子心中十分疑惑……這個星球這麼小，那個國王到底能統治些什麼呢？

　　「陛下，」他對國王說：「抱歉！請容許我提個問題——」

　　「我命令你提出問題。」國王立刻鄭重宣布。

　　「陛下——你統治些什麼？」

　　「一切！」國王簡潔有力地回答。

　　「一切？」

　　國王比比自己的星球，又比比別的星星，還有所有的星星。

　　「全部？」小王子問。

　　「全部！」國王回答。

　　因為他的統治權不僅絕對，並且遍及整個宇宙。

　　「那些星星都服從您嗎？」

　　「當然服從，」國王說：「他們毫不猶豫地服從。我絕不允許任何人違抗命令的。」

　　小王子對這樣的權力簡直驚歎之至。要是他也擁有這樣的威勢，就可以好好的看夕陽了。不是一天四十四次，而是七十二次、一百次，甚至兩百次，連椅子都不用移。想到被自己遺棄的那顆小星星，小王子忽然覺得有點傷心。於是，他鼓起勇氣向國王討個人情。

　　「我好想看夕陽……求您垂愛……命令太陽下山……」

　　「要是我命令某個大將像蝴蝶一般在花間飛來飛去、或者寫齣悲劇、或者變化成海鳥，而大將卻不肯遵行這個命令時，錯的是哪個？」國王問：「是大將，還是我？」

　　「是您！」小王子斷然表示。

　　「沒錯！要求別人做什麼事，必須考慮他能否辦得到。」國王接下去說：「接受權威首重合理。假若你要人民跑到海邊去跳海，他們會起來鬧革命。我之所以有權要求人民服從，是因為我的命令合理。」

　　「那麼我的夕陽呢？」小王子提醒國王。他是一有問題，絕不輕易了事的。

「你看得到落日；我會下命令。不過，依據我的管理技巧，
必須等到狀況合適時才行。」

　「那要等到什麼時候？」小王子詢問。

　「嗯嗯！」國王先是拿起一本又厚又重的大曆書研究一番，
這才答道：「嗯……嗯！大約——大約——約莫在傍晚七點四十
分左右；屆時你就可以看到我的子民有多聽話
了。」

　　小王子又打呵欠了。看不到落日，他很懊
惱。而且，他開始覺得無聊了。

「我在這兒沒別的事做，」他對國王說：「所以我要再度起程了。」

「別走！」國王好不容易有個子民，心中覺得十分自傲，忙說：「別走！我讓你當部長。」

「什麼部長？」

「司──司法部長！」

「可是這裏沒人可審哪！」

「這還不曉得哩！」國王告訴他：「我還沒巡視過整個王國。我年紀大了，這裏沒個地方可以停馬車，要我走路又實在太累了。」

「哦！可是我看過了呀！」小王子又回頭瞄瞄星球的另一邊。那邊和這邊如出一轍，根本沒人……

「那麼，你可以審判自己。」國王回答：「那可是全天下最難的事。審判自己比審判別人難多了。要是你可以自我審判成功，就可以稱得上是真正的智者啦！」

「是啊！」小王子說：「不過，我到哪裏都可以審判自己，未必非留在這個星球上不可。」

「嗯！嗯！」國王說：「我有充分的理由可以認定在我的星球上的某個角落裏，還住著一隻老耗子；我夜裏聽見牠的聲音。你可以審判這隻老耗子，隨時都可以判牠死刑。這樣，牠的生命就全憑你的執法存續了。不過，你要每次都饒恕牠；不能跟牠太計較，牠可是我們唯一的子民嗽！」

「我，」小王子答道：「我不喜歡判任何人死刑。還有，我想我現在就要上路了。」

「不行！」國王說。

可是小王子已經準備好要離開，無心為老國王擔憂了。

「要是陛下希望我能立即服從，」他說：「就該給我合理的命令。比方說，你可以命令我在一分鐘內離開，這似乎比較合於情理……」

小王子見國王沒答話，猶豫了一下，然後歎口氣舉步離去。

「我命令你當我的特使。」國王趕緊大呼。

依舊是十足權威模樣。

「大人們真是好奇怪。」小王子繼續他的旅程，一面走，一面喃喃自語。

11

第二個星球上住著一個自大狂。

「哇！哇！有個崇拜者要來拜訪我嘍！」他才看到小王子往這方向走，便遙遙高呼著。

因為，自負的人總以為別人都把自己視為偶像。

「早安！」小王子打個招呼：「你頭上戴的帽子真古怪。」

「這是答禮用的。」自大狂回答：「人們向我喝彩時，我就舉帽致意。可惜，這條路一直沒人路過。」

「是嗎？」小王子根本不明白自大狂說的是怎麼一回事。

「鼓掌，別停。」這時自大狂指揮他。

小王子開始鼓掌，而自大狂則鄭重其事地舉帽答禮。

「這比拜訪國王有意思多

了。」小王子默想。於是他開始一次又一次地鼓掌，那自大狂便一次又一次地重複舉帽致意。

這樣持續了五分鐘，小王子漸漸對這個單調無聊的遊戲感到不耐煩了。

「要怎樣才能讓你放下帽子呢？」他問。

可是自大狂根本沒聽到；自負的人除了讚美外，一向是聽不到任何話語的。

「你真的非常崇拜我嗎？」他問小王子。

「『崇拜？』──什麼意思啊？」

「崇拜就是你認為我是這星球上最英俊、最體面、最有錢、最聰明的人。」

「但你是這星球上唯一的人啊！」

「好心點，還是要照樣崇拜我嘞！」

「我崇拜你！」小王子輕輕聳聳肩：「可是，這有什麼好讓你那麼高興的呢？」

然後，小王子就走了。

「大人們的確是很奇怪！」他繼續踏上旅程，一面走、一面自言自語。

12

下一個星球上住的是個酒鬼。這次訪問過程很短暫，卻使小王子心情十分頹喪。

「你在那兒做什麼？」小王子發現在一大堆空瓶子及一大堆滿滿的瓶子前，有個人靜靜坐在那兒，便問那人。

「我在喝酒。」酒鬼老實地回答。

「為什麼要喝酒呢？」小王子追問。

「這樣我才能遺忘。」酒鬼答稱。

「遺忘什麼？」小王子心裏已經開始替他難過了。

「遺忘我的恥辱。」酒鬼心中惘然，垂下了頭。

「什麼恥辱？」小王子窮問不捨。他想幫助酒鬼。

「喝酒的恥辱！」酒鬼說完這話，就閉口不肯再說任何一字一句了。

於是，小王子滿腹疑團地走了。

「大人們的確是非常、非常地怪異。」他繼續踏上旅程，一面走、一面自言自語。

13

　　第四個星球是屬於一名實業家的。這人忙得不得了，以致小王子到達時，他連頭都沒擡一下。

　　「早安！」小王子問候他：「你的菸熄了。」

　　「三加二等於五。五加七等於十二。十二加三等於十五。早！十五加七等於二十二。二十二加六等於二十八。我沒空再點火了。二十六加五等於三十一。唔！這樣一來就有五億零一百六十二萬兩千七百三十一顆嘍！」

　　「五億顆什麼？」小王子問。

　　「咦?!你還在呀？五億零一百──我不能中斷……我有好多事要做！我在進行重要的事，沒空跟你囉嗦。二加五等於七……」

　　「五億零一百萬顆什麼？」小王子又重複著那個問題；這輩子他還沒輕易放棄任何疑問過。

　　實業家擡起頭來：

　　「我在這個星球上住了五十四年了，只被打擾過三次。第一次是在二十年前，不知打哪兒掉了一隻昏了頭的鵝來。牠那叫聲啊，擾得四下都是回音，吵死人了，害得我加錯數目。第二次在十一年前，我患了風濕痛；因為運動量不夠──我沒時間到處逛嘛！第三次──喂！就是現在啦！我剛剛算到……五億零一百萬──」

　　「零一百萬什麼？」

　　實業家這下總算明白了，只要他不回答這個問題，就休想有片刻安寧。

　　「五億零一百萬個小東西。」他說：「天上看得到的東西。」

「蒼蠅嗎？」

「喔！不！是發亮的小東西。」

「蜜蜂嗎？」

「喔！不是，不是。是金色的小東西，可以讓懶人做春秋大夢的東西。至於我呢！我正在進行重要大事，沒空做那些白日夢。」

「啊！你指的是星星。」

「沒錯，就是星星。」

「那麼你數這五億顆星星做什麼呢？」

「五億零一百六十二萬兩千七百三十一顆，我在進行重要的事：我講求要精確。」

「那麼，你到底數這些星星做什麼？」

「我數它們做什麼？」

「是啊！」

「沒什麼！我擁有它們。」

「你擁有這些星星？」

「沒錯！」

「可是我見過一個國王，他——」

「國王他們並不算真的擁有，他們只算統治而已；這是完全不同的。」

「那麼，你擁有這些星星，又有什麼用呢？」

「這可以令我富有。」

「富有又能做什麼呢？」

「富有的話，等有新星星被發現時，我就可以買下來啦！」

「這個人，」小王子默想：「跟那個可憐的酒鬼倒是有幾分相像。」

不過，他還有更多疑問哩！

「一個人怎麼可能擁有那些星星呢？」

「那麼，它們又是屬於誰的呢？」實業家氣急敗壞地反問。

「我不曉得，不屬於任何人吧！」

「所以，它們就該屬於我才對，因為我是第一個想到這一點的人。」

「有必要嗎？」

「當然有。當你發現一顆不屬於任何人的鑽石時，它就是你的。當你發現一座無主的島嶼時，它也是你的。當你領先他人，想到一個新主意時，便可以申請專利，它是你的了。而我正是如此；由於我在別人都沒想過要擁有它們之前，先想到這個主意，所以我擁有這些星星。」

「是嘛！話是不錯！」小王子說：「但你擁有它們之後，又能如何呢？」

「我可以管理它們，三番兩次地計算數目。」實業家回答：「這事不容易；還好，我天生對重要的事就有興趣。」

小王子還是不滿意。

「如果我擁有一條絲巾，」他說：「我可以把它繫在脖子上戴著走。如果我擁有一朵花，我也可以把它摘下來帶在身邊。但是，你沒辦法把星星從天上摘下來……」

「哦！當然不行。不過，我可以把它們放在銀行裏。」

「什麼意思?!」

「意思是說：我會把我的星星的數目寫在一張紙片上，然後把紙片放在某個抽屜裏鎖起來。」

「就這樣？」

「這樣就夠了。」實業家說。

「真有趣！」小王子想：「的確頗富詩意。不過，這並不是什麼了不得的事呀！」

小王子心目中所謂重要的事，和大人們觀念中重要的事，是不大相同的！

「我自己本身就擁有一朵花。」他接著和實業家交談：「我每天都幫她澆水。我還有三座火山，每個禮拜都會把它們清理乾淨（包括一座死火山也一同清理；誰也不知道它以後會怎樣嘛！）我的火山多少有點用處，我的花也一樣；所以我才擁有它們。可是，那些星星對你沒什麼用……」

實業家張大了嘴，卻無話可答，而小王子則逕自走了。

「大人們的確都很怪裡怪氣。」他繼續前進，並對自己簡短地說了一句。

14

　　第五個星球非常特別。那是小王子沿路看到最小的一顆，整個星體上只容得下一盞路燈和一名燈夫。小王子實在想不出，在天空的某個角落，一個沒有人、沒有房子的星球上，需要一盞路燈、一名燈夫做什麼？不過，他依舊默默地跟自己說：

　　「這人或許是十分荒唐可笑。不過，總比那國王、自大狂、實業家都好得多了。至少，他的工作有意義。每當他點燃那盞路燈時，就彷彿為一顆星星、一朵花帶來生命；而當他想熄滅燈火時，同時也為花兒、星星帶來睡眠。這是個美麗的行業；因美而真正有用的行業。」

　　抵達那顆星球時，他滿懷敬意地向那位燈夫行禮。

　　「早安！您為何要把街燈熄滅了呢？」

　　「那是規矩。」燈夫回答：「早安！」

　　「什麼規矩啊？」

　　「規矩是我得熄掉這盞燈。晚安！」

　　然後，他又點上燈。

　　「那你剛剛為什麼又要點上燈呢？」

　　「那是規矩嘛！」燈夫回答。

　　「我不懂。」小王子說。

　　「沒什麼好不懂的，」燈夫說：「規矩就是規矩。早安！」

　　接著又熄了燈，然後拿出一條紅色方格手帕來擦拭額頭。

　　「我從事這一行真是恐怖！從前是很合理：早上熄燈，傍晚點燈；白天其他時間我可以鬆弛一下，晚上也能睡覺。」

　　「那以後規矩就變了嗎？」

　　「規矩沒變，」燈夫說：「這才真叫悲劇哩！年復一年，這個星球愈轉愈快，而規矩卻依舊沒變！」

・我從事的這一行太恐怖了

「後來——後來到了現在，這個星球每分鐘就轉一圈，我連想要喘一秒鐘氣都不成。每一分鐘，我都得把燈點亮再熄掉！」

「那可真是好玩！在你住的這個地方，一天才只有一分鐘而已！」

「這一點兒也不好玩！」燈夫說：「我們剛剛說話的時候，就已經過了一個月啦！」

「一個月？」

「沒錯，一個月。三十分鐘，等於三十天。晚安！」

他再度點起燈。

小王子看著他，覺得自己挺喜歡盡忠職守的燈夫。他想起從前想要追尋落日時，只須搬動椅子便行了；所以，他想幫助這位朋友。

「嗨！」他說：「我可以教你一個辦法，讓你隨時想休息，就可以休……」

「我一直就盼望能休息。」燈夫說。

盡責的人，可能也會常常想偷懶一下哦！

小王子接下去說明：

「你的星星夠小的了，只要跨三步就可以走完一圈。要是你希望永遠陽光普照，只須慢慢、慢慢地往前直走就行嘍。只要你想休息，就開始走路——那麼，你希望白天有多長，它就有多長。」

「這對我沒什麼好處，」燈夫說：「我最渴望的是睡眠。」

「那你太倒楣了。」小王子說。

「我真的很倒楣。」燈夫說：「早安！」

接著又把燈熄了。

「那個人，」小王子又踏上旅程，一路想著：「或許會被其他所有的人：國王、自大狂、酒鬼、實業家……等瞧不起。不過，不管怎麼說，他是這些人當中，唯一不會令我感到荒謬的。或許，這是因為他不是只顧自己，而還能想到其他方面事情的緣故吧！」

他傷感的嘆了口氣，再次自言自語起來：

「那人是我見過這些人當中，唯一值得交朋友的一個。可惜，他的星球實在太小了，沒有足夠的空間可以同時容納兩個人……」

小王子所悵於承認的是：離開那個星球，比什麼都教他難過；因為那地方頗受上蒼眷顧，每天可以看到一千四百四拾個落日。

15

第六個星球比上一個還大上十倍，上面住著一位撰寫大部頭書籍的老紳士。

「喲嗬！有個探險家來嚕！」他望見小王子走來，便自顧自地嚷嚷起來。

小王子坐在桌邊，胸口兀自微微起伏：這一路行來，可走得真遠、真久！

「你是打哪兒來的？」老人家問他。

「那邊那一大本書是什麼？」小王子不答又問：「你是做哪一行的？」

「我是個地理學家。」對方回答。

「地理學家又是什麼？」小王子問道。

「地理學家嘛！地理學家就是個知道一切海洋、河川、城鎮、山陵以及荒漠的人。」

「那可真有意思。」小王子說：「總算見到一個有真正職業的人啦！」他逡巡地理學家的星球一遍，發現是他迄今所見到最壯觀瑰偉的一顆星。你的星球好漂亮，」他說：「這個星球上有任何海洋嗎？」

「我無可奉告。」地理學家說。

「哎呀！」小王子很失望：「有山脈嗎？」

「我無可奉告。」地理學家又說。

「那麼有城市、河流、荒漠嗎？」

「我還是無法告訴你。」

「可是你是地理學家啊！」

「正是！」地理學家又說：「但我不是探險家；我連個星球都沒探勘過。當個地理學家，並不需要出去統計城市、河流、山脈、海洋以及沙漠有多少？地理學家有比到處遊蕩更重要的事做。他不用離開自己的書桌，而是從探險家那邊吸收知識，問他們問題，將他們旅遊中的記憶記錄下來。若是其中哪個探險家的資料能勾起他的興致，他便要仔細追究對方的道德人品了。」

「為什麼呢？」

「因為，萬一那名探險家說了謊，或者喝酒喝過了頭的話，就會使地理學家的書遭受牽連了。」

「那又為什麼？」小王子問。

「因為酒醉的人容易看到重影。這樣一來，地理學家便會把原本只有一座山的地方，記載成有兩座山啦！」

「我就認識一個人，」小王子說：「他鐵定是位很差勁的探險家。」

「那是有可能的。接下來，若是探險家的人品沒問題，我們就會仔細探究他的發現。」

「找人去查看一番嗎？」

「个！那太瑣碎了。只是，地理學家必須要求探險家提出證據。比如說：如果我們要探究的，是他所發現的一座山，便會要他帶塊那座山中的人石頭來。」

那名地理學家陡然激奮起來：

「而你──你來自遙遠的地方！你是個探險家！你該把你的星球形容給我聽的！」

地理學家打開大記事簿、削尖了鉛筆等著。探險家的敘述一向是先用鉛筆記下來，等到證據齊備之後，才會以墨水筆正式登錄。

「準備好了嗎？」地理學家滿心期盼地說。

「喔！我住的那個地方，並非十分有趣。」小王子說：「那地方什麼東西全是小小的。我有三座火山；兩座是活火山，一座已經熄了。不過，天曉得未來又會是如何？」

「誰也不會曉得的。」地理學家說。

「我還有一朵花兒。」

「我們不記錄花的。」地理學家說。

「為什麼？那朵花可是我整個星球上最漂亮的東西嘞！」

「我們不記載這些，」地理學家回答說：「因為它們全是朝生暮死的。」

「『朝生暮死？』──什麼意思呢？」

「地理上，」地理學家說：「一切書籍只記載重大事物，這些事物永遠不會過時。要一座山脈改變位置，或要一片汪洋自行枯涸，都是亙古難得一見的。我們所記載的，也就是這些永恆的事物。」

「可是，即使是死火山，也可能有復活的時候，」小王子打斷他的話：「『朝生暮死』又意味著些什麼？」

「管它是火活山、死活山，」地理學家說：「對我們來說，它總是一座山，這是不變的。」

「可是，『朝生暮死』到底是什麼意思呢？」小王子反反覆覆地問。他一旦提出問題，就絕不善罷干休。

「那是說：『有很快就會消失的危險！』」

「我的花很快會有消失的危險嗎？」

「正是。」

「我的花是朝生暮死的。」小王子自言自語地說：「她只有四個刺可以自衛，來對抗整個世界。而我⋯⋯我卻把她孤零零一個留在我的星球上！」

這是他第一次感到後悔。不過，他很快就又再度恢復了勇氣。

「現在，你建議我去拜訪什麼地方呢？」他問。

「地球！」地理學家答覆：「它的名聲很不錯。」然後，小王子便一路想著他的花，離開了這個星球。

16

所以，這第七個星球就是地球嘍！

地球可不是一顆平凡的星球！仔細算算，那上頭有一百一十一位國王（千萬別忘了，其中還包括黑人領袖）、七千名地理學家、九十萬個商人、七百五十萬個酒鬼、三億一千一百萬個自大狂──也就是說，總數約有二十億名成年人。

為了讓諸位對地球的大小有個概念，我可以告訴您：在人們還沒發明電力以前，地球上的六大洲必須集結四十六萬二千五百一十一名的燈夫大軍，才足以確保點燃所有的街燈。

由稍遠的地方望去，這幅景象可真光彩絢爛。這隊燈夫的行動，被規劃得宛如歌劇院裏的巴蕾舞團一般。

最先出場的是紐西蘭和澳洲的燈夫，他們點亮燈後，就退場睡覺去了。接下去步入舞臺的是中國和西伯利亞的燈夫，然後又揮軍退居幕後。而後是蘇俄和印度的燈夫現身，再來是非洲和歐洲，接著是南美洲，最後則是北美。他們從不會搞錯燈臺的次序，氣勢可真壯闊。

唯有負責照料北極那管孤零零的街燈，以及照料南極之燈的兩名燈夫——他們過得安逸而閒散；因為，這兩人一年僅須忙碌兩次就夠了。

17

一個人想要賣弄聰明時，有時便會有偏離事實的時候。關於燈夫的事，我說的並非十分坦誠。而我明白，這很可能會使不了解我們這個星球的人產生錯誤的觀念。人類在地球上佔據的地方還很小；若是兩百萬居民像參加群眾聚會時一般擠在一塊兒的話，也只須二十哩見方的面積便可以容得下這些人了。而全球的人類，只要太平洋上一個小島就可以裝載得下啦！

一旦你把這些事實告訴大人，他們是絕不可能聽信的。他想像自己佔有很大的空間，幻想自己和大木棉一般重要。所以嘍，你就該建議他們，自己好好計算一下吧！不過，您本身可千萬別浪費時間做這件多餘的工作；這是不必要的。我知道，你會相信我的。

小王子到達地球時沒見到任何人，心中覺得驚詫萬分。當月光灑向大地，在黃沙上滾起一道金邊時，他開始懷疑自己是否走錯星球了。

「晚安！」小王子懇懇地問候。

「晚安！」一條蛇說。

「我是到哪個星球來了呢？」小王子問。

‧你是一條有趣的動物……不比一根手指粗……

「你到地球來啦！這裏是非洲。」蛇回答。

「啊！那麼地球上沒有人嗎？」

「這裏是沙漠，沙漠是沒有人的；地球可大著哩！」蛇說。

小王子坐到一塊石頭上，攪頭望向天空。

「我真納悶，」他說：「星星之所以在天上閃得這麼亮，是不是為了讓我們每個人，到了某一天都能再找回自己的星……瞧我的星球，它就在我們頭頂上方，卻又離得那麼遠！」

「它真漂亮！」蛇說：「你為什麼跑到這裏來呢？」

「我和一朵花兒之間出了點問題。」小王子說。

「啊！」蛇驚呼，兩個人都緘默了下來。

「人都到哪兒去了？」小王子終於重拾話題：「沙漠裏有點寂寞……」

「跟人在一起還是寂寞。」蛇說。

小王子直盯著牠看，好久才說了一句：「你是條有趣的動物……不比一根手指粗……」

「可是，就算國王的手指，也沒我這麼大的能耐。」蛇說。

小王子笑了。

「你並不是很有能耐，你連腳都沒有，就算要旅遊也不行……」

「我能帶你到任何船都走不到的地方。」蛇說。

牠纏繞在小王子足踝上，宛若個金鐲子一樣。

「無論哪個人，只要讓我碰一下，便能送他到他的故土去。」蛇又說：「而你卻是如此誠摯又純真，並且是來自某個其他的星球……」

小王子沒搭腔。

「你令我同情 —— 在這花崗岩形成的地球上，你是太柔弱了。」蛇說：「萬一哪天你患了思鄉病，想再回到自己的星球，我可以幫助你。我可以——」

「哦！我非常了解。」小王子說：「但你為什麼說話老像在做猜謎呢？」

「這些謎由我來解。」蛇說。

然後，兩人都不做聲了。

18

　　小王子橫越沙漠時，只遇到　朵花。那朵花有三個花瓣，一點都不起眼。

　　「早安！」小王子說。

　　「早安！」花兒說。

　　「人們都在哪兒呢？」小王子彬彬有禮地問。

　　花兒曾見一個商隊經過。

　　「人們？」她回應了一聲：「我想，約莫還有六、七個吧！幾年前我見過他們；不過，誰也不曉得該到哪裏去找這些人。他們沒有根，因此生活起來備嘗艱辛。」

　　「再見！」小王子說。

　　「再見！」花兒說。

19

　　之後，小王子登上一座高山。以前他所知道的山，僅限於他那三座火山而已。它們只有他的膝蓋高，常被他用來當腳凳。「在這麼高的山上頭，」他自言自語：「我一眼就可以看遍整個星球，以及所有的人……」

　　可是，這兒除了湖泊和如針般尖銳的岩石外，他什麼也看不到。

　　「早安！」他禮貌地說。

　　「早安──早安──早安。」回聲回答。

　　「你是誰？」小王子說。

　　「你是誰──你是誰──你是誰？」回聲又答。

　　「跟我交朋友，我好孤獨。」他說。

　　「我好孤獨──我好孤獨──好孤獨！」回聲飄蕩依舊。

　　「多奇怪的星球啊！」他心想：「什麼都是乾乾尖尖的。而且這裏的人完全沒想像力，人家說什麼就跟著說什麼……在我的星球上，我有一朵花，每次都是她先開口……」

‧這個星球到處都是乾乾的，稜稜角角的！

20

還好，越過沙漠、岩石與雪地後，小王子終於來到一條道路上。只要有路，就會通往人類的住所。

　　「早安！」他說。

　　這時，他站在一座花園前，園裏清一色是玫瑰花。

　　「早！」玫瑰們問候。

　　小王子凝望著她們；她們看起來全和他的花兒相仿。

　　「妳們是誰呀？」他震驚不已。

　　「我們是玫瑰。」玫瑰花兒回答。

　　他傷心透了。他的花兒曾經告訴他，放眼全宇宙，再也找不到一個她的同類啦！而在此地，僅僅是一座花園內，就有五千朵和她一模一樣的花了。

　　「要是她看見這……」他默想：「心裏一定煩死了。她一定會咳得好厲害，裝作快要死了的模樣，免得被人笑話。而我啊！

我只得裝模作樣地安慰她，好讓她恢復元氣──因為，我若是不肯這麼委曲求全的話，她真會結束生命的……」

他一個勁兒地追懷：「我自以為擁有世上獨一無二的花、富裕非凡；想不到她卻只是一朵普普通通的花而已。一朵半凡的玫瑰花、三座到我膝蓋高的火山──而且其中一座，或許永遠不會再活動了……我不是個很偉大的王子……」

然後便趴在草地上大哭了起來。

‧小王子趴在草地上大哭起來……

21

就在這個時候，狐狸出現了！

「早哇！」狐狸說。

「早！」小王子禮貌地回敬；轉過頭來，卻看不到任何人。

「我在這兒呢！」那聲音道：「就在蘋果樹下。」

「你是誰呀？」小王子問完，又補充一句：「你看起來好漂亮哦！」

「我是隻狐狸。」狐狸答道。

「過來和我玩玩吧！」小王子提議：「我心情好壞喲！」

「我不能跟你玩，」狐狸說：「我還沒被馴服哪！」

「哦！真抱歉。」小王子說。

可是，他想來想去，又追問一句：

「『馴服?!』──什麼意思啊？」

「你一定不是住在這裏的。」狐狸說：「你在找什麼呢？」

「我在找『人』。」小王子又說：「『馴服』究竟是什麼意思呀？」

「人啊！」狐狸說：「他們有長槍打獵，挺擾人的；他們還飼養雞隻；這些是他們僅有的興趣。你在找雞嗎？」

「不是。」小王子又道:「我在找尋朋友;『馴服』到底是什麼意思哪?」

「那是一種常被忽視的行為,」狐狸告訴他:「意思就是「造成約束」。」

「造成約束?」

「正是。」狐狸表示:「對我而言,你不過就是個丁點兒大的小男孩,跟其他上千百個男孩子沒什麼兩樣。我對你無所求,而你呢?就你來說,也無求於我。對你而言,我就跟其他無數狐狸一樣,僅是一隻狐狸而已。然而,一旦你馴服了我,我們就將互有需求了。對我而言,在世上,你是獨一無二的,對你呢?我也是世上的唯一……」

「我漸漸明白些了,」小王子說:「有一朵花……我想她已經馴服我了。」

「這很有可能,」狐狸說道:「地球之上,什麼事都可能發生。」

「哦!不!這事不是發生在地球上!」小王子說。

狐狸好像被搞迷糊了,一副十分好奇的樣子。

「在另一個星球上?!」

「沒錯!」

「那個星球上有獵人嗎?」

「沒有!」

「喲嗬!太棒啦!有雞吧?」

「也沒有。」

「唉!天下沒有十全十美的事。」

狐狸歎了口氣;卻又立刻轉回到自己的念頭上:「我的生活真是單調乏味;我獵雞,人們又獵我。所有的雞都一樣,所有的人類也都一模一樣。結果是,我有點厭倦了。不過,若是你馴服了我,那我的生命就彷彿出現了陽光。我會在雜沓的腳步聲中,辨識出某一個聲響。聽到別人的腳步聲,我會趕緊躲回地下去。

若是你的腳步聲,則會像音樂般,召喚我走出藏身之窟。唉!看到那邊那片麥田了嗎?好可惜!我不吃麵食,小麥田對我是一點用處也沒有,也談不上任何意義。然而,你的頭髮是金黃色的。想想,一旦你馴服了我,那將有多美妙呀!望著那金黃色的麥田,會讓我想起你。而我也將愛上聆聽麥浪翻飛的聲音……」

牠凝視著小王子,良久、良久……

「請──請馴服我!」他說。

「我是很想,非常非常想。」小王子回答說:「可是我時間不多。我得去發現朋友,還得去了解許多事情呢!」

「除了所馴服的事物以外,人們一無所知。」狐狸說:「人類沒有多餘的時間去了解任何事情。他們在商店裏購買現成的東西,卻找不到任何一些商店可買到友誼。因此,人們再也沒有朋友了。要是你想有個朋友，就馴服我吧！」

「想馴服你，得先要做些什麼？」小王子問。

「你得非常有耐心。」狐狸答覆：「最初，你得坐在離我稍遠的地方 —— 就像那樣 —— 坐在草地上。我會先用眼角餘光瞄你，這時你可別說任何話，語言是誤會的根源。不過，你得一天天坐得離我愈來愈近……」

第二天，小王子再度回到這地方。

「若是你在每天同樣的時間來更好。」狐狸告訴他：「比方說，你下午四點來，那麼三點鐘時我就會開始興奮起來。而且，

・「如果你在下午 4 點鐘來的話，那麼到了 3 點左右，我就會開始興奮起來了。」

時間愈近，我就愈高興。一等到四點呢，我就會焦躁不安、急得跳腳了。我會讓你知道我有多快活！不過你要是任何時間都可能來，我就不曉得什麼時間該準備好歡迎你的心情了……。是人，就該有自己獨特的儀式……」

「儀式是什麼啊！」小王子問。

「那也是常被人忽略的行為，」狐狸說：「是使每一天、每一刻各異其趣的緣由。例如，搜捕我的獵戶間有個儀式；每到禮拜四都和村子裏的女郎跳舞。因此，對我來說，禮拜四可真是個大好日子！我可以一直散步到葡萄園那頭去。然而，一旦獵戶們隨時都可能開舞會的話，那每個日子就都是一個模樣了，而我也就連個假期都沒有嘍！」

於是，小王子馴服了狐狸。而等到他離去時辰逼近時……

「唉！」狐狸說：「我要哭了。」

「是你自己的錯，」小王子說：「我從沒指望過要傷害你，可是你卻希望我馴服你……」

「是啊！就是說嘛！」狐狸應和著。

「那麼，這一切對你根本沒有好處嘛！」

「有好處，」狐狸說：「那是來自於麥田的顏色。」接下去牠又補充說：

「再去看看那些玫瑰花；現在，你會了解你的玫瑰是獨一無二的了。然後回來跟我道再會，我將會送你一個祕密做為禮物。」

小王子遂再度走過去瞧那些玫瑰花。

「妳們一點都不像我那朵玫瑰，」他說：「妳們至今仍無足輕重。沒人馴服過妳們，而妳們也不曾馴服過任何人，就和我當初剛碰到時的狐狸沒兩樣。牠跟其他千百隻狐狸原本相仿，但我讓牠成了我的朋友。此後在這世上，牠是獨一無二的了。」

玫瑰們聽了感覺好窘、好羞慚。

「妳們長得很漂亮，但卻只是空殼子。」他侃侃而談：「沒有人會要為妳們而死。想當然，一般陌生人會認為我的玫瑰——屬於我的那朵玫瑰——和妳們一模一樣。而事實上，她本身卻比妳們這些無數的玫瑰都重要多了。因為：我為她澆過水、蓋過玻璃罩、遮過屏風、撲殺過毛毛蟲（不過我留下其中兩、三隻，讓牠們蛻變為蝴蝶）；因為我曾聆聽著她抱怨、吹噓、甚或沈默。因為，她是我的玫瑰。」

然後，他回去見狐狸。

「再會！」他說。

「再會！」狐狸說：「現在我把那祕密說出來，其實很平凡。人，只有用心靈才能看得透澈，事物的精髓，光憑眼睛是看不到的。」

「事物的精髓，光憑眼睛是看不到的。」小王子複述一次，以便牢牢記住。

「是你為你那玫瑰所耗費的時間，使她變得如此重要。」

「是我為我那玫瑰所耗費的時間……」小王子為記住這話，再次唸道。

「人們已然忘記這個真理，」狐狸說：「但你不能忘。對於你已馴服的對象，你永遠負有責任。就像你必須對你的玫瑰花負責……」

「我必須對我的玫瑰花負責。」小王子又跟著唸了一遍，好讓這句話深印在腦海中。

22

「早安！」小王子打了個招呼。

「早安！」鐵路轉轍手也說。

「你在這裡做什麼？」小王子問。

「我為千把個成群的旅人分發。」轉轍手答道：

「我分派運送他們的火車：時而往左、時而往右。」

這時一列亮麗的快車響聲如雷、飛馳而過，把轉轍手的小茅屋震得一顫一顫的。」

「跑得好急啊！」小王子說：「他們在追尋什麼呢？」

「這個嘛！就連列車長也不知道他們在追尋什麼哩！」轉轍手說。

第二列鮮亮的快車又自另一個方向飛馳而過。

「他們已經回來了嗎？」小王子探究。

「這不是先前的那一列，」轉轍手說：「那些人們的路線正好相反。」

「他們對於自己原本的地方不滿意嗎？」小王子問。

「沒有人會對自己所在的地方滿意的。」轉轍手說。

接著，他們又聽到第三列飛快車的震天聲響。

「他們是在追逐第一部列車的旅客嗎？」小王子追問。

「他們沒追逐什麼。」轉轍手說：「他們要不是在裏頭睡覺，就是在打呵欠。只有孩子們才會把鼻子壓在玻璃窗上往外張望。」

「只有孩子才知道他們在追尋什麼。」小王子說：「他們會把時間花在一個破破爛爛的娃娃上，而這娃娃對他們便顯得重要了；要是有人想把它拿走的話，孩子們就要哭了……」

「孩子們是有福的。」轉轍手說。

23

「早安！」小王子說。

「早安！」商人說。

那是位賣止渴藥丸的商人。這藥丸只要每星期服用一粒，就不會再想喝別的東西了。

「你為什麼要賣這些呢？」小王子問。

「因為專家曾經計算過，」商人表示：「吃這些藥丸可以省下許多時間；一星期可以省下五十三分鐘了。」

「那麼，這五十三分鐘該用來做什麼呢？」

「隨你的意……」

「我嘛……」小王子默唸：「若是我有五十三分鐘可以隨意運用，我要優哉遊哉地漫步到一道清涼的泉水那頭去。」

24

自從在沙漠出了意外，到這時已是第八天了。聽完那商人的故事，同時我也喝掉了身邊的最後一滴水。

「唉！」我對小王子說：「你的回憶確實十分動人，問題是我到現在既沒有修好飛機，身上也沒水喝了。若是我也能優哉遊哉地蕩到清涼的泉水邊，我也會非常高興的！」

「我那狐狸朋友——」小王子有話要告訴我。

「我親愛的小人兒，眼前可沒有什麼事能跟狐狸扯上關係的喲！」

「這又為什麼？」

「因為我就快渴死了……」

他沒搞懂我為什麼這麼說，卻回答：

「即使快死了，曾經有一個朋友也是好事。好比說我吧！我就很高興曾經擁有過狐狸這麼個朋友……」

「老天！他對我的危機根本沒概念。」我心想：「他沒餓過、沒渴過，他只需要一絲絲的陽光就夠了……」

而他定定地望著我，解答我心中的思緒：

「我也渴了，讓我們一塊兒去找口井吧……」

我委實疲憊不堪。在一望無際的沙漠中，漫無目標地尋找一口井，簡直是荒唐嘛！不過，不管怎麼說，我們還是出發了。

跋涉了幾個鐘頭後，夜幕已然低垂，星星也開始一顆顆高掛天際。我渴得有點頭昏眼花，眼望星星，恍若置身夢境一般，小王子的話在腦海中晃晃盪盪……

「你是說，你也渴嗎？」我追問。

但他並沒有回答我的問題，只對我說：

「水對心靈應當也有好處……」

這種答案我無法理解，卻也沒說什麼。我清楚得很，要想再從他口中掏出什麼答案來，是比登天還難。

他累了，坐了下來，我則挨著他身邊坐下。這樣靜靜坐了一陣子後，他又開口了：

「星星好美！因為，在繁星間有一朵看不見的花兒。」

我答道：「是啊！的確是。」便望著月光下綿延無際的沙脊，不再多說什麼。

「沙漠好美！」小王子又說。

他說的沒錯。我一向就喜歡沙漠；坐在荒漠中的沙丘上，看不到任何東西、聽不到任何聲音。然而,在幽靜的深處,有某個東西在悸動著、閃爍著……

「沙漠之所以會美,」小王子表示:「是因為其中某個地方隱藏著一口水井……」

猝然了解到沙漠中那神祕的光輝,令我心生驚異。當還是個小男孩時,我住在一幢老屋裏,傳說那屋中埋著某種寶藏。當然,沒有人知道該如何將它挖掘出來;或許根本沒有人去找過那批寶藏。但傳說卻使這房子令人著迷;在我家深處,即埋藏著一個祕密……

「是的,」我告訴小王子:

「那房子、繁星、沙漠——之所以美,美在肉眼看不見的地方!」

「真高興你同意那狐狸的話。」

小王子睡著了;我抱起他,再度往前走。我內心深深感動,血脈為之澎湃,彷彿自己抱著的,是一件極為脆弱的珍寶。甚至,我心裏覺得,在整個地球上,再也找不到比他更纖弱的寶物了。月光下,我瞧著他蒼白的額、緊閉的眼,以及在風中輕顫的捲髮,對自己說:「此地,我所見到的不過是具軀殼;而最重要的部分,光用眼睛是看不見的……」

他雙唇微微張著,嘴角掛著朦朧的笑意。

我再度對自己說:「熟睡中這位小王子,令我如此深深感動的,是他對某朵花兒那份忠貞的愛——這朵玫瑰的影像,照亮了他整個生命,彷彿一盞明燈那般,甚至在他熟睡的時候……」

而我竟覺得他更脆弱了。我有股想要保護他的衝動,好似他本身就是一道微風吹過便可能熄滅的火花……

這麼走著、走著,破曉的時候,我找到水井了。

「人們，」小王子說：「坐上快車就往前走，卻不知道自己在追尋什麼。他們莽莽撞撞、情緒激昂，一直兜圈子⋯⋯」

　　然後，他又多加一句：

　　「不需要這麼麻煩的⋯⋯」

　　我們找到的這口井，跟一般撒哈拉沙漠中的井不一樣。撒哈拉沙漠中的水井，通常只是在沙漠中挖個洞就算了，這口井倒像村莊裏的井。然而，這裏並沒有村莊。於是我想，我一定是在做夢⋯⋯

　　「真奇怪，」我對小王子說：「什麼事都替我們準備得好好的：滑輪、吊桶、繩索⋯⋯」

　　他笑笑，摸了摸繩子，然後啟動滑輪。滑輪咔滋、咔滋地響著，恍如早被風兒遺忘的老風信雞一樣。

　　「聽到了嗎？」小王子說：「我們喚醒了水井，此時它正唱著歌⋯⋯」

　　我可不希望他為了拉繩子而把自己累壞了。

　　「讓我來，」我說：「這些東西對你來說太重了。」

　　我緩緩地將吊桶升到井邊擺好──完成這工作，我是既累又高興。那滑輪的歌聲依舊在我耳際縈迴，同時，我可以看到陽光在微波輕漾的水面閃爍。

　　「我好渴望喝喝這水，」小王子說：「也請給我一點兒水喝⋯⋯」

　　而我了解他一直在追尋些什麼。

　　我把吊桶攙到他唇邊，他閉上眼睛喝著，那水是如此甘甜，似是某種不凡的款待。而它確實不同於一般的滋養品；它的甘甜來自於星光下的奔走、滑輪的歌唱，以及我雙臂的努力。它可以滋潤心靈，彷彿一件禮物一樣。當我還是個小男孩的時候，聖誕樹上的小燈、午夜的彌撒樂、溫柔的笑臉，都增添了我所收到那些禮物的光芒。

「你生活周遭的人，」小王子說：「在一座花園中種了五千朵玫瑰——而他們卻無法自其中找到他們所要追尋的東西。」

「他們真的找不到。」我答道。

・他笑笑，摸了摸繩子，然後啟動滑輪。

「然而他們一直在追尋的東西，其實只是在一朵花兒上，或在幾滴水之間就可以找得到的。」

「是的，真的是這樣。」

小王子接著又說。

「但肉眼是盲目的，人們必須用心靈去尋找……」

我喝了水，呼吸暢快多了。日出時候，沙漠成了蜂蜜般的色調，而這蜂蜜色調也令我心歡暢。那麼，又是什麼帶給我這憂傷的感覺呢？

「你得遵守你的諾言。」小王子坐回我身邊，柔聲地說。

「什麼諾言？」

「就是——為我的羊畫個口罩……我得對我的花兒負責……」

我從口袋裏把所有草圖掏出來，小王子一一看過，大笑著說：

「你畫的木棉——看起來有點像包心菜哩！」

「是嗎！」

我一直很以那幅木棉為傲的。

「你畫的狐狸——耳朵有點像號角，而且也太長了。」

然後，他又笑了。

「小王子，你說這話不公平。」我抗議：「除了畫蟒蛇吞象的內在圖和外觀圖外，我完全不曉得該怎麼畫別的東西呀！」

「哦！沒關係的，」他說：「孩子們看得懂的。」

於是，我又用鉛筆畫了個口罩。把畫遞給他的時候，我的心好亂。

「你有我不曉得的計畫？」我說。

他卻沒回答，只告訴我：

「你知道——我降落到地球……到明天就一週年了。」

接著，他沈默了一會兒，繼續說：

「我降落的地點離這裏很近。」

他臉紅了。

不知為什麼，那股莫名的憂愁再度襲上我的心頭。有個問題忽然浮現腦海：

「這麼說來，那天清晨初次見到你，並不是偶然的嘍——一個禮拜前——你就像那般，一個人慢慢地晃，從數千里外有人煙的地方，孤單單地走來？你是要走回最初著陸的地方嗎？」

小王子臉又紅了。

找心中有幾分遲疑，可終究又追問了一句：

「或許是因為一週年的關係吧？」

小王子的臉再度紅起來。他沒有回答任何問題，但是——當一個人臉紅時，豈不就表示默認了嗎？

「啊？」我告訴他：「我有點震驚——」但他打斷了我的話。

「現在，你必須工作了，你得回去修理你的引擎。我會在這裏等你，明天黃昏時再回來……」

我心情卻沒因此而放鬆，我憶起了那隻狐狸。倘若一個人被馴服了的話，就得冒可能揮淚的險。

26

井邊有一堵坍塌了的老石牆。第二天黃昏，我工作完畢回到此地時，遠遠地就望見小王子坐在石牆頂端，一雙腳掛在那邊晃來晃去。我聽見他說：

「看來你是忘了，這裏並不是正確的地點。」

想必有另一個聲音回答了他的話，因為他又答道：「正是！正是！就是這一天，卻不是這地方。」

我繼續走向牆邊，沒再聽見什麼，也沒有看到任何東西。然而，小王子卻又回答：

「——就是這樣,你會在沙地上看到我動身的足跡。你只要等著我就成了;晚上我到那裏去。」

這時,距離牆邊只有二十米遠了,我還是沒看到任何東西。

沈寂了一會兒,小王子又說:

「你有好毒藥嗎?你確定它不會使我痛苦太久?」

我停下腳步,一顆心都快碎了,卻還是聽不懂。

「該走啦!」小王子說:「我要從牆上跳下來了。」

我往下細瞧,望向牆角邊——我跳了起來!在我眼前,面對著小王子的,是一條足以在三十秒內令人致命的小黃蛇。我一面往後退、一面從口袋中掏出左輪手槍。然而,那條蛇聽見了我的聲音,一下子像一道落地泉水般靈活地鑽入沙地中,發出微微聲響,自石縫間消失無蹤。

我及時趕到牆邊,伸手接住小王子;他的臉色蒼白得像雪一樣。

「怎麼回事?」我問他:「你為什麼跟蛇講話?」

我鬆開他一向繫在頸邊的圍巾,弄濕他的太陽穴,給他喝點水。這時,我再也不敢問他任何問題了。他鄭重地望著我,手摟著我的脖子;我覺得他的心跳,有如一隻被來福槍打到、瀕臨垂死邊緣的小鳥一般。

「真高興你已經找出引擎的毛病了,」他說:「現在你可以回家了——」

「你怎麼知道的。」

我才正要告訴他,我的工作進行得十分順利,遠超乎我原本的指望哩!

他沒答覆我的話,反而接下去說:

「今天,我也要回家了……」然後傷感地加了一句——

「這路程,遠好多……困難好多……」

我清楚地意識到,某件非比尋常的事正在進行著。我用雙臂緊緊擁抱著他,好像他還是個小娃兒一樣。然而,我依舊感覺他像是要一頭衝向幽冥地府，而我卻無力阻止……

他神情嚴肅，彷彿十分迷惘。

「我有了你畫的羊，又有給羊住的房子，還有個口罩……」

然後，他對我做出一個悲傷的笑容。

我等了好久，感覺到他正一點一點地振作起來。

「親愛的小人兒，」我對他說：「你在害怕……」

無庸置疑地，他是真的害怕。不過，他卻愉快地笑著。

「小人兒，」我說：「我好想再聽聽你的笑聲。」

但他卻對我說：

「今晚，就是一週年了……屆時，我可以在一年前初抵地球

・該走啦……我要從牆上跳下去了。

的地點上空，找到我那顆星星……」

「小人兒，」我說：「告訴我這只是個惡夢──這條蛇、這會晤之地、這星星都只是……」

而他卻不曾回答我的請求，只是對我說：

「真正重要的東西，光憑肉眼是看不到的……」

「是的，我知道……」

「就好比那朵花一樣。如果你愛上一朵長在某顆星星上的花，夜裏凝望星空都會覺得甜蜜無比。滿天的星星，都像盛開著花兒……」

「是的，我知道……」

「又好比那井水一樣。只因為那滑輪、那繩索，你給我喝的水就變得有如樂聲那般。可還記得──那滋味有多甜美！」

「是的，我知道……」

「夜晚，你可以抬頭望望星星。我住的地方，一切事物都是那麼小，所以我沒辦法告訴你怎麼找到那顆星。或者，這樣更好。對你而言，我的星星只是群星中的一顆。也因此，你會喜愛看天空中的每一顆星星……它們都會成為你的朋友。此外，我將送給你一個禮物……」

他又笑了起來。

「啊！小王子，親愛的小王子！我真愛聽這笑聲！」

「這便是我的禮物。就像這樣，這笑聲將會像我們喝井水時那樣……」

「你試圖說明些什麼呢？」

「所有的人都有星星。」他說：「但對不同的人而言，它們卻有不同的含義。對旅人而言，星星是他們的嚮導；對另外一些人來說，它們就只是夜空中的小明燈了；對學者來說，它們是待解的謎題；對我見過的實業家而言，它們又代表著財富；但是所有的星星都是沈默的。你──唯有你──所擁有的星星和別人都不同──」

「你是想說明什麼呢？」

「在無數星星中的某一顆上，我就住在上頭笑著。因此，當你仰望夜空的時候，就彷彿天上星星都在笑一般……你——唯有你——將擁有會笑的星星。」

然後，他又笑了。

「而當你憂傷平息後（時間會紓解一切憂傷），你會為曾認識我而心滿意足。你永遠是我的朋友，永遠與我同歡笑。有時候，你會打開窗口，找尋那段歡樂……或許，你的朋友看到你望著天空笑，會感到十分驚奇。到時候，你會對他們說：『不錯，星星總是勾起我的笑意！』而他們則會認為你瘋了；這可是我對你耍的一個卑鄙小把戲喲……」

他再一次笑了起來。

「這就有如在群星閃爍的天際，我給了你許許多多會笑的小鈴鐺一樣……」

於是，他又笑了，然後迅即轉為凝重：

「今夜——你……你……別來。」

「我不會離你而去。」我說。

「我看起來會像很痛苦，好像快死了一樣。別來看那幅景象，不值得這麼麻煩……」

「我不離開你。」

但他卻很擔心。

「告訴你吧——這或許也是由於蛇的關係。我不能讓牠咬到你！蛇是冷血動物，牠或許只為一時興起，便會咬你……」

「我不離開你！」

這時，他忽然想起：

「對了！牠們沒有餘毒可以再多咬人一口。」

當晚我沒看見到他動身；他了無聲息地離我而去。我趕上他的時候，他正快速而堅決地往前走，只對我說了一句：

「啊！你來了……」

他握著我的手，卻依舊擔心。

「你不該來的，那會教你難受。我看起來會像死了一樣，但那不是真的……」

我沒搭腔。

「你知道的……距離太遠了，我沒辦法帶著軀殼回去，它太重了。」

・他像一棵大樹緩緩倒下，沒有一絲聲響……

我沒說話。

「但那就彷彿被丟棄的軀殼，對於一具舊軀殼，是沒有什麼好悲傷的……」

我沒出聲。

他有些氣餒，卻仍鼓起剩餘的那一點勇氣：

「你曉得，那將是很美好的；因為，我也將凝視星星，而每顆星星都像那銹了滑輪的井一樣，都會掏出水給我喝……」

我沒答話。

「那會很有意思的！你將擁有五億個小鈴鐺，而我將擁有五億口清水井……」

他也無法說下去了；因為，他哭了……

「到了！讓我自己走吧！」

他坐了下來，因為他心裏害怕。然後，他又說：

「你懂的 —— 我的花……我必須對她負責。而她是如此脆弱，如此天真！她只有四根刺，要用來保護自己，而抵抗這世界，是一點也派不上用場的……」

我也坐了下來，因為，我再也站不住了。

「而今 —— 這就是一切……」

他還是有點遲疑，但仍舊站了起來，往前邁了一步，而我卻無法動彈了。

那邊，在他的腳踝只不過有一些黃光。有段時間，他仍一動不動地挺立在那裏。他沒有叫，就像一棵大樹那樣、緩緩倒了下來，連一絲聲響都沒有。因為，那是沙地。

27

而今，時隔六年了……我從未提起這故事。見到我生還，平日的夥伴都放下心來。我很傷心，但只告訴他們：「我累了。」

現在，我的憂傷平復些了；換句話說——並不完全。不過，我曉得他已經回到自己的星球上；因為，天亮後我找不到他的軀體。那並非很重的軀體……入夜，我喜愛聆聽星子聲，就彷彿是五億顆小鈴鐺……

然而，還有件出乎意料的事……當我為小王子畫那口罩時，忘了為它加條皮帶子，他不可能把它繫在他的綿羊身上了。所以，我一直不敢確定：他的星球上現在如何？說不定綿羊會吃了他的花……

有時，我告訴自己：「當然不會！小王子每天晚上都會幫他的花兒蓋上玻璃罩，並且會十分謹慎地看好那綿羊……」於是，我便覺得高興，繁星的笑聲也就顯得特別悅耳。

　　但有時我又會跟自己說：「萬一又有疏忽，那一切就完了！要是某天晚上他忘了蓋好玻璃罩；或者綿羊跑了出來，在夜裏、靜悄悄地……」這時，那些小鈴鐺便化成滾滾珠淚了……

　　因之，對於諸位也喜愛小王子的人，以及對我這視他為獨一無二的人而言，這是極為神奇的事。在我們不知道的某個地方，有隻從未謀面的綿羊，是或否，已經吃掉了一朵玫瑰……

　　仰望星空，問問自己：是或否？綿羊是否已吃掉了那朵花兒？然後，你會發現，一切事物都在改變……

　　而永遠沒有一個成人能了解，這件事是多麼、多麼重要啊！

　　這幅畫，是我心中最喜愛、也最神傷的景觀。它跟前頁那幅一模一樣，再畫它，只為加深諸位的印象。那是小王子出現在地球上的地方，也是他消失的地方。

　　仔細看看它，或許，某天你到非洲沙漠遊歷時，就會認得這個地方。同時，倘若你到了這地方，請不要來去匆忙。就在那星星之下停留一段時光吧！那麼，倘若有個小人兒笑著現身，他長著金黃捲髮、拒絕回答任何問題，你就會認得他了。若有一天，這情況真的出現了，請捎來他返回的訊息，安慰安慰我這思念的心靈吧！

〈全書終〉

譯者後序

這本具有高度智慧的童話小說，是由法國的聖·修伯里所著。他於一九〇〇年六月二十九日在法國里昂出生，而於一九四四年七月三十一日的地中海戰線上消失了蹤影。

他於二十歲左右起，即對飛行產生了濃厚的興趣，甚至遭遇數次危險仍不退縮，因此，形成了他異於常人且高於常人的價值觀。他的作品，如《南方郵政機》（一九二九）、《夜間飛行》（一九三一）或《人間大地》等，都被視為是難得一見的名著經典。

讀者們認為，由於他能遨遊空中、縱橫飛行，使得他視物更為清晰，作品更異於一般作家，充滿了高度的智慧與內涵。

本書是由巴黎的加利馬社於一九四六年，將聖·修伯里遺作中的一卷作品翻譯後刊行的。獻身於飛行的作者認為，雖然小王子所居住的星球是那麼小，但他仍然選擇回到那如明玉般清澈美麗的故鄉這件事，是非常合理的。因此，當作者於飛機上凝視夜空，看見單獨發光的可愛小星星時，眼中就會浮現出那位自然、純真的小王子。另一方面，作者由高空中觀看地球時，也領悟到世間的悲苦人類往往不追求事物真理，甚至以錯為真的無知行為等等。《小王子》中隱含著許多超越童話的精髓及作者的生活經驗；書中的幻想和不經意的對話，更包含了許多對人類生命、生活哲理各方面都極為重要的事物及觀念。

作者曾說：「每個人都是由小孩子成長為大人的。然而，多數的大人們卻不記得這件事。」今日的社會，孩子們的純真已不復見，個個都想一躍而成為大人；成人們任意擺出的大人架子令人厭煩，其對事物產生的許多無知的曲解，更令人不敢苟同。然而，不管人間世事如何改變，仍有許多成人不失其赤子之心。所以，經由此書的闡述，便可窺知今日社會的癥結，乃在於喪失自然性。因此聖‧修伯里著作此書的目的，就是要人們找回失去的童心，尋回真正的自我。另外要讓孩子及人們知道，一直能保持赤子之心的大人，才是真正的成人。這本內容意義深遠、發人省思的寓言式童話故事，是值得您一讀再讀、細細品味的。

　　經過現實的洗禮後，任何人都很輕易地會回憶起從前的美好。因此，少年時代的生活，便會經常地浮現在腦海中。

　　由此可知，並不只是聖‧修伯里能回到孩童時代，人們的成年與少年時代都是接續著的，在今與昔之間，必須靠心才能來回的行走，所以，對於過去，我們只能以追尋來肯定它的存在。

　　而作者於書中所提到的，人有許多令人討厭之處的看法，雖然也有人認同，但卻無人將它寫出。另外，此書中運用許多任意畫出的插圖，更是無人使用過的，這兩點，都可說是此童話故事引人入勝的地方。

　　在此，也許我們並不認為那令我們毫不在意的起伏綿延的沙地，和從高空望去的小星星有多麼的美，然而，在一位日日以繪圖為工作的畫者心中，那種美的價值卻是無可比擬的。

　　所以，一位出世者的單純及入世者的狹窄、苦悶，可說是兩個永遠無法交集的世界。

關於（作者）聖・修伯里

「聖・修伯里是個飛行家。幾乎一生都在空軍飛行員生涯中度過的聖・安東尼，遨遊於空中、凝視著世界及人們，並累積心中的一點一滴，創造出《小王子》，同時飛往白雲的彼岸，再也沒有回來。」

各式各樣的傳說

不論最初的寫作動機為何，《小王子》雖是作者聖・修伯里基於逃離現實社會、回歸童話世界的心態而著，但是絕沒有要讀者重返童話世界的意思。

作者於一九四二年夏天開始執筆，當時他正亡命於紐約，為了使戰敗的法國復甦而四處奔走，但是對於政治家猶疑不定的心態，他深感失望，於是興起遠渡美國、從國外救法國的念頭。

但是，在那裏，他看到的是置祖國、人類、文明的危機於不顧，而互相敵對的黨派抗爭。他絕望之餘，索性將自己孤立起來，不料卻因此遭到別人惡意的中傷。

在那段失意不斷的日子裏，他經常到咖啡店裏，想著要是有像「小王子」那樣的小孩，將多麼令人安慰，所以，他經常在餐巾紙上，以描繪「小王子」的草圖來掩蓋內心的寂寞。他被推薦在兒童讀物上撰寫類似的少年讀物，於是，《小王子》誕生了。他第一件事就是去買色筆。隨著無數的草圖練習，想要寫的內容也越來越清晰。他拒絕了專業畫家的建議，認為將自己的思想率直地表現出來才最重要。

人們通常追尋可當作聖誕節禮物的童話或充滿夢境、幻想、美麗事件及愉快事物的童話。的確在這故事中，星星、王子、玫瑰花、狐狸、蟒蛇、燈夫及國王等等，均熱鬧地陸續登場，但是他們卻沒有經常在故事中出現成為達成人們夢想及願望的希望精靈及喜劇式的結果。

他一直對於寫作兒童讀物的構想很著迷，並積極熱心地著手進行，但是「適合兒童」意味著什麼？難道是蒐集兒童們所喜愛的，能掌握他們情緒的就是適合兒童？他並不這麼認為。

有一點經常被誤解——他雖說要重視兒童，但並不是放手不管小孩。對他來說，孩子的成長及其過程都必須要有價值，而對培育此種價值的存在，則必須使用嚴格的精神教育。所以兒童讀物並不是要討好兒童，而是要打動兒童的內心。

由於覺得回歸戰鬥部隊的時候近了；無論如何，他要將這本書作為給孩子們的遺言。使他們不會成為招惹世界危機的那般成人；他盡心盡力地闡述必須要能看透、認清事物的重要性，及必須用心去體會的任何事情。到底是什麼樣的危機？他以吞象的蟒蛇，描繪出當時大概每隔六個月就會燃起侵略軍事行動的德國。

這本書與一般童話最大的區別，就是在天真爛漫的故事背後，不斷地感受到悲壯的堅強情緒與故事情節。

「因為我太年輕，所以不知道要珍惜那朵花。」

「我將住在那些星星中的一個上面，並在那上面微笑。」

小王子重複地說這句話，也暗示著他（飛行員）在向其妻子及親友道別離。

　　我認為這本書能夠持續不斷地吸引眾多讀者的原因，不在於她相當優秀的詩及哲學或文學的作品，而是她隱藏了作者面對死亡的決心及與親人離別的祕密。

家世與生平

　　聖・修伯里，於一九○○年六月二十九日，以法國舊貴族的長子身分誕生於里昂。四歲時父親過世，在慈母的愛護下，與桑莫力斯頓、雷蒙及拉莫爾等，在母親親戚的莊園中，度過了幸福的孩提時代。

　　他從小就喜歡機械，隨著　九○三年末萊特兄弟的成功，對開始展開的飛行機時代也抱著濃厚的興趣，他曾將舊床單綁在柳枝的骨幹上，將其固定在腳踏車上滑行。十二歲時也曾試乘過當時有著蝙蝠翅膀般羽翼的飛機。

　　從學校畢業後，由於他對海洋憧憬，所以把海軍學校當成目標，可惜在口試時失敗。服兵役時，進入了航空隊擔任候補幹部，學習飛機的操作，自此踏出了空中飛行的第一步。退伍後，過了一段不合本意的薪水階級生活。一九二六年，進入民間的航空公司為拉提葛艾爾工作，擔任郵政機的飛行員，由法國的杜爾茲起飛，經西班牙、順著撒哈拉沙漠的大西洋沿岸南下，從卡薩布蘭加、達喀爾延伸的路線，在嚴酷的風土、不完備的機體及萬一不小心著陸會被莫爾人俘虜的惡劣條件下，歷練成為一名沈穩勇敢的飛行員。以孤獨死於沙漠中之飛行員的冒險愛情故事為主題的《南方郵政機》，就是以這段時期的體驗為基礎所寫成的作品。

　　征服非洲之後，他被派遣至南美去實現愛爾波斯塔爾公司的大計畫。首先，整頓南美的航空網；之後，橫越大西洋，經由非洲將南美和歐洲連結起來。聖・修伯里越過安地斯山脈，確立了連接巴西和智利的安利・基歐面及夜間的飛行，然後與以商業機首先橫渡大西洋的姜・美露莫茲並列，開拓從布宜諾斯艾利斯至南美大陸之最南端的巴塔哥尼亞路線，保存了先驅者不滅的功績。第二步作品《夜間飛行》（一九三一年法密拉獎）即是描述當時與黑夜、荒天、山岳相格鬥之飛行員的奮鬥故事。

之後，愛爾波斯塔爾公司宣告破產。對聖・修伯里來說，這是他流浪時代的開始，只能做個試飛駕駛員及新聞雜誌投稿者。巴黎至西貢間的長距離飛行失敗、不小心降落在利比亞沙漠及瓜地馬拉的失速事件，都是在這段時期發生的。在這些故事發生後的療養生活中所寫的《人間大地》（一九三九年，阿卡提米大賞）裏，他道出了自己的體驗，也展現了歷經人生教訓後思想成熟的文體。

第二次世界大戰一開始，他就擔任偵察機的成員，並執行多次的危險任務。休戰後曾一度到了美國。敘述實地參加阿拉斯加上空偵察飛行的《戰鬥飛行員》，於一九四二年出版，又是他人在美國時所作。聯合國的反擊一開始，他就下定決心向位於非洲的原來部隊歸隊。而成為永遠最暢銷書的《小王子》（一九四三年）就是他前往非洲前不久時出版的。

向原部隊歸隊後，他駕駛著當時最新銳的機種，雙機腹的P38，執行法國上空的照相攝影偵察，並且從不拒絕任何危險的任務。

一九四四年七月三十一日，聖・修伯里從可爾斯加基地出發，偵察包括出生地里昂及靠近孩童時代居住之莊園附近的亞努斯。也就是這次任務，使他再也沒有回來過。根據多項資料及證據顯示，他在舉行結婚典禮的亞紀莊園附近，曾遭受德國敵機的攻擊，而墜落於地中海。這個結局實可說是最符合《小王子》作者的命運。

聖‧修伯里年鑑

1900年　6月29日，誕生於法國里昂。

1912年　暑假，成為在當時被稱為國家英雄的飛行員。第一次乘坐飛機。

1920年　海軍學校考試失敗。10月進入美術學校建築科就讀。

1921年　4月，受徵召服役。第二年取得民間飛行員、空軍飛行員資格。

1926年　1月，處女作《飛行員》刊載於『銀之船』雜誌。

1929年　《南方郵政機》出版。

1931年　4月，與康斯艾諾‧蘇絲結婚。《夜間飛行》出版，得到法密拉獎。

1935年　4月末至5月，以『巴黎‧索瓦爾』報紙特派記者的身分，駐在莫斯科。由聖‧修伯里編劇的電影〈安紐瑪利〉上映。

1939年　2月，出版《人間大地》。獲得阿卡提米小說獎。9月英法對德開戰應召入伍。

1942年　2月，出版《戰鬥飛行員》。夏天，開始著手寫《小王子》。

1943年　2月，出版《給某一人質的信》。4月6日《小王子》出版。6月晉升少校。

1944年　7月31日，執行古魯諾布魯及亞努斯方面的高空偵察。8點45分從基地出發後，就沒有再回來……

1998年　有漁船在馬賽外海，撈到刻有「聖修」的手環。

2003年　10月法國文化部請來的打撈公司將刻有「2734」的飛機殘骸撈上岸來，與修伯里的軍中編號吻合，研判這即是修伯里的失事飛機……

"I believe that for his escape he took advantage of the migration of
a flock of wild birds."

The Little Prince

WRITTEN AND DRAWN BY

ANTOINE DE SAINT-EXUPÉRY

1

Once when I was six years old I saw a magnificent picture in a book, called *True Stories from Nature*, about the primeval forest. It was a picture of a boa constrictor in the act of swallowing an animal. Here is a copy of the drawing.

In the book it said : " Boa constrictors swallow their prey whole, without chewing it. After that they are not able to move, and they sleep through the six months that they need for digestion."

I pondered deeply, then, over the adventures of the jungle. And after some work with a coloured pencil I succeeded in making my first drawing. My Drawing Number One. It looked like this :

I showed my masterpiece to the grown-ups, and asked them whether the drawing frightened them.

But they answered : " Frighten? Why should any one be frightened by a hat?"

My drawing was not a picture of a hat. It was a picture of a boa constrictor digesting an elephant. But since the grown-ups were not able to understand it, I made another drawing : I drew the inside of the boa constrictor, so that the grown-ups could see it clearly. They always need to have things explained. My Drawing Number Two looked like this :

The grown-ups' response, this time, was to advise me to lay aside my drawings of boa constrictors, whether from the inside or the outside, and devote myself instead to geography, history, arithmetic and grammar. That is why, at the age of six, I gave up what might have been a magnificent career as a painter. I had been disheartened by the failure of my Drawing Number One and my Drawing Number Two. Grown-ups never understand anything by themselves, and it is tiresome for children to be always and forever explaining things to them.

So then I chose another profession, and learned to pilot aeroplanes. I have flown a little over all parts of the world; and it is true that geography has been very useful to me. At a glance I can distinguish China from Arizona. If one gets lost in the night, such knowledge is valuable.

In the course of this life I have had a great many encounters with a great many people who have been concerned with matters of consequence. I have lived a great deal among grown-ups. I have seen them intimately, close at hand. And that hasn't much improved my opinion of them.

Whenever I met one of them who seemed to me at all clear-sighted, I tried the experiment of showing him my Drawing Number One, which I have always kept. I would try to find out, so, if this was a person of true understanding. But, whoever it was, he, or she, would always say :

" That is a hat."

Then I would never talk to that person about boa constrictors, or primeval forests, or stars. I would bring myself down to his level. I would talk to him about bridge, and golf, and politics, and neckties. And the grown-up would be greatly pleased to have met such a sensible man.

2

So I lived my life alone, without anyone that I could really talk to, until I had an accident with my plane in the Desert of Sahara, six years ago. Something was broken in my engine. And as I had with me neither mechanic nor any passengers, I set myself to attempt the difficult repairs all alone. It was a question of life or death for me : I had scarcely enough drinking water to last a week.

The first night, then, I went to sleep on the sand, a thousand miles from any human habitation. I was more isolated than a shipwrecked sailor on a raft in the middle of the ocean. Thus you can imagine my amazement, at sunrise, when I was awakened by an odd little voice. It said :

" If you please——draw me a sheep!"

" What!"

" Draw me a sheep!"

I jumped to my feet, completely thunderstruck. I blinked my eyes hard. I looked carefully all around me. And I saw a most extraordinary small person, who stood there examining me with great seriousness. Here you may see the best portrait that, later, I was able to make of him. But my drawing is certainly very much less charming than its model.

That, however, is not my fault. The grown-ups discouraged me in my painter's career when I was six years old, and I never learned to draw anything, except boas from the outside and boas from the inside.

Now I stared at this sudden apparition with my eyes fairly starting out of my head in astonishment. Remember, I had crashed in the desert a thousand miles from any inhabited region. And yet my little man seemed neither to be straying uncertainly among the sands, nor to be fainting from fatigue or hunger or thirst or fear. Nothing about him gave any suggestion of a child lost in the middle of the desert, a thousand miles from any human habitation. When at last I was able to speak, I said to him :

" But —— what are you doing here ?"

And in answer he repeated, very slowly, as if he were speaking of a matter of great consequence :

" If you please——draw me a sheep..."

When a mystery is too overpowering, one dare not disobey. Absurd as it might seem to me, a thousand miles from any human habitation and in danger of death, I took out of my pocket a sheet of paper and my fountain-pen. But then I remembered how my studies had been concentrated on geography, history, arithmetic and grammar, and I told the little chap (a little crossly, too) that I did not know how to draw. He answered me :

" That doesn't matter. Draw me a sheep..."

But I had never drawn a sheep. So I drew for him one of the two pictures I had drawn so often. It was that of the boa constrictor from the outside. And I was astounded to hear the little fellow greet it with,

" No, no, no! I do not want an elephant inside a boa constrictor. A boa constrictor is a very dangerous creature, and an elephant is very cumbersome. Where I liver, everything is very small. What I need is a sheep. Draw me a sheep."

So then I made a drawing.

He looked at it carefully, then he said :

" No. This sheep is already very sickly. Make me another."

So I made another drawing.

My friend smiled gently and indulgently.

" You see yourself," he said, " that this is not a sheep. This is a ram. It has horns."

So then I did my drawing over once more. But it was rejected too, just like the others.

" This one is too old. I want a sheep that will live a long time."

By this time my patience was exhausted, because I was in a hurry to start taking my engine apart. So I tossed off this drawing.

And I threw out an explanation with it.

"This is only his box. The sheep you asked for is inside."

I was very surprised to see a light break over the face of my young judge : "That is exactly the way I wanted it! Do you think that this sheep will have to have a great deal of grass?"

" Why?"

" Because where I live everything is very small..."

" There will surely be enough grass for him," I said. " It is a very small sheep that I have given you."

He bent this head over the drawing :

" Not so small that—— Look! He has gone to sleep..."

And that is how I made the acquaintance of the little prince.

3

It took me a long time to learn where he came from. The little prince, who asked me so many questions, never seemed to hear the ones I asked him. It was from words dropped by chance that, little by little, everything was revealed to me.

The first time he saw my aeroplane, for instance (I shall not draw my aeroplane; that would be much too complicated for me), he asked me:

" What is that object ? "

" That is not an object. It flies. It is an aeroplane. It is my aeroplane."

And I was proud to have him learn that I could fly.
He cried out, then :

" What! You dropped down from the sky?"

" Yes," I answered, modestly.

" Oh! That is funny!"

And the little prince broke into a lovely peal of laughter, which irritated me very much. I like my misfortunes to be taken seriously.

Then he added :

" So you, too, come from the sky! Which is your planet?"

At that moment I caught a gleam of light in the impenetrable mystery of his presence ; and I demanded, abruptly : "Do you come from another planet ?" But he did not reply. He tossed his head gently, without taking his eyes from my plane :

" It is true that on that you can't have come from very far away..."

And he sank into a reverie, which lasted a long time. Then, taking my sheep out of his pocket, he buried himself in the contemplation of his treasure.

You can imagine how my curiosity was aroused by this half-confidence about the " other planets." I made a great effort, therefore, to find out more on this subject.

" My little man, where do you come from ? What is this 'where I live,' of which you speak ? Where do you want to take your sheep ?"

After a reflective silence he answered :

" The thing that is so good about the box you have given me is that at night he can use it as his house."

" That is so. And if you are good I will give you a string, too, so that you can tie him during the day ; and a post to tie him to."

But the little prince seemed shocked by this offer :

" Tie him! What a queer idea!"

" But if you don't tie him," I said, "he will wander off somewhere, and get lost."

My friend broke into another peal of laughter :

" But where do you think he would go ?"

The Little Prince on Asteroid B-612

" Anywhere. Straight ahead of him."

Then the little prince said, earnestly :

" That doesn't matter. Where I live, everything is so small !"

And, with perhaps a hint of sadness, he added :

" Straight ahead of him, nobody can go very far..."

I had thus learned a second fact of great importance : this was that the planet the little prince came from was scarcely any larger than a house!

But that did not really surprise me much. I knew very well that in addition to the great planets—such as the Earth, Jupiter, Mars, Venus—to which we have given names, there are also hundreds of others, some of which are so small that one has a hard time seeing them through the telescope. When an astronomer discovers one of these he does not give it a name, but only a number. He might call it, for example, "Asteroid 325."

I have serious reason to believe that the planet from which the little prince came is the asteroid known as B-612.

This asteroid has only once been seen through the telescope. That was by a Turkish astronomer, in 1909.

On making his discovery, the astronomer had presented it to the International Astronomical Congress, in a great demonstration. But he was in Turkish costume, and so nobody would believe what he said.

Grown-ups are like that...

Fortunately, however, for the reputation of Asteroid B-612, a Turkish dictator made a law that his subjects, under pain of death, should change to European costume. So in 1920 the astronomer gave his demonstration all over again, dressed with impressive style and elegance. And this time everybody accepted his report.

If I have told you these details about the asteroid, and made a note of its number for you, it is on no account of the grown-ups and their ways. Grown-ups love figures. When you tell them that you have made a new friend, they never ask you any questions about essential matters. They never say to you, "What does his voice sound like? What games does he love best? Does he collect butterflies?" Instead, they demand: "How old is he? How many brothers has he? How much does he weigh? How much money does his father make?" Only from these figures do they think they have learned anything about him.

If you were to say to the grown-ups : " I saw a beautiful house made of rosy brick, with geraniums in the windows and doves on the roof," they would not be able to get any idea of that house at all. You would have to say to them : " I saw a house that cost £ 4000." Then they would exclaim : " Oh, what a pretty house that is !"

Just so, you might say to them : "The proof that the little prince existed is that he was charming, that he laughed, and that he was looking for a sheep. It anybody wants a sheep, that is a proof that he exists." And what good would it do to tell them that? They would shrug their shoulders, and treat you like a child. But if you said to them : " The planet he came from is Asteroid B-612," then they would be convinced, and leave you in peace from their questions.

They are like that. One must not hold it against them. Children should always show great forbearance toward grown-up people.

But certainly, for us who understand life, figures are a matter of indifference. I should have liked to begin this story in the fashion of the fairy-tales. I should have liked to say : " Once upon a time there was a little prince who lived on a planet that was scarcely any bigger than himself, and who had need of a friend..."

To those who understand life, that would have given a much greater air of truth to my story.

For I do not want any one to read my book carelessly. I have suffered too much grief in setting down these memories. Six years have already passed since my friend went away from me, with his sheep. If I try to describe him here, it is to make sure that I shall not forget him. To forget a friend is sad. Not every one has had a friend. And if I forget him, I may become like the grown-ups who are no longer interested in anything but figures...

It is for that purpose, again, that I have bought a box of paints and some pencils. It is hard to take up drawing again at my age, when I have never made any pictures except those of the boa constrictor from the outside and the boa constrictor from the inside, since I was six. I shall certainly try to make my portraits as true to life as possible. But I am not at all sure of success. One drawing goes along all right, and another has no resemblance to its subject. I make some errors, too, in the little prince's height : in one place he is too tall and in another too short. And I feel some doubts about the colour of his costume.

So I fumble along as best I can, now good, now bad, and I hope generally fair-to-middling.

In certain more important details I shall make mistakes, also. But that is something that will not be my fault. My friend never explained anything to me. He thought, perhaps, that I was like himself. But I, alas, do not know how to see sheep through the walls of boxes. Perhaps I am a little like the grown-ups. I have had to grow old.

5

As each day passed I would learn, in our talk, something about the little prince's planet, his departure from it, his journey. The information would come very slowly, as it might chance to fall from his thoughts. It was in this way that I heard, on the third day, about the catastrophe of the baobabs.

This time, once more, I had the sheep to thank for it. For the little prince asked me abruptly—as if seized by a grave doubt—" It is true, isn't it, that sheep eat little bushes ?"

" Yes, that is true."

" Ah ! I am glad !"

I did not understand why it was so important that sheep should eat little bushes. But the little prince added :

" Then it follows that they also eat baobabs ?"

I pointed out to the little prince that baobabs were not little bushes, but, on the contrary, trees as big as castles ; and that even if he took a whole herd of elephants away with him, the herd would not eat up one single baobab.

The idea of the herd of elephants made the little prince laugh.

" We would have to put them one on top of the other," he said.

But he made a wise comment :

"Before they grow so big, the baobabs start out by being little."

"That is strictly correct," I said. "But why do you want the sheep to eat the little baobabs ?"

He answered me at once, "Oh, come, come !" , as if he were speaking of something that was self-evident. And I was obliged to make a great mental effort to solve this problem, without any assistance.

Indeed, as I learned, there were on the planet where the little prince lived—as on all planets—good plants and bad plants. In consequence, there were good seeds from good plants, and bad seeds from bad plants. But seeds are invisible. They sleep deep in the heart of the earth's darkness, until some one among them is seized with the desire to awaken. Then this little seed will stretch itself and begin—timidly at first — to push a charming little sprig inoffensively upward toward the sun. If it is only a sprout of radish or the sprig of a rose-bush, one would let it

grow wherever it might wish. But when it is a bad plant, one must destroy it as soon as possible, the very first instant that one recognizes it.

Now there were some terrible seeds on the planet that was the home of the little prince ; and these were the seeds of the baobab. The soil of that planet was infested wit them. A baobab is something you will never, never be able to get rid of if you attend to it too late. It spreads over the entire planet. It bores clear through it with its roots. And if the planet is too small, and the baobabs are too many, they split it in pieces...

"It is a question of discipline," the little prince said to me later on. "When you've finished your own toilet in the morning, then it is time to attend to the toilet of your planet, just so, with the greatest care. You must see to it that you pull up regularly all the baobabs, at the very first moment when they can be distinguished from the rose-bushes which they resemble so closely in their earliest youth. It is very tedious work," the little prince added, "but very easy."

The Baobabs.

And one day he said to me : " You ought to make a beautiful drawing, so that the children where you live can see exactly how all this is. That would be very useful to them if they were to travel some day. Sometimes," he added, " there is no harm in putting off a piece of work until another day. But when it is a matter of baobabs, that always means a catastrophe. I knew a planet that was inhabited by a lazy man. He neglected three little bushes..."

So, as the little prince described it to me, I have made a drawing of that planet. I do not much like to take the tone of a moralist. But the danger of the baobabs is so little understood, and such considerable risks would be run by anyone who might get lost on an asteroid, that for once I am breaking through my reserve. " Children," I say plainly, " watch out for the baobabs !"

My friends, like myself, have been skirting this danger for a long time, without ever knowing it ; and so it is for them that I have worked so hard over this drawing. The lesson which I pass on by this means is worth all the trouble it has cost me.

Perhaps you will ask me, " Why there are no other drawings in this book as magnificent and impressive as this drawing of the baobabs ?"

The reply is simple. I have tried. But with the others I have not been successful. When I made the drawing of the baobabs I was carried beyond myself by the inspiring force of urgent necessity

6

Oh, little prince ! Bit by bit I came to understand the secrets of your sad little life...For a long time you had found your only entertainment in the quiet pleasure of looking at the sunset. I learned that new detail on the morning of the fourth day, when you said to me :

" I am very fond of sunsets. Come, let us go look at a sunset now."

" But we must wait," I said.

" Wait ? For what ?"

" For the sunset. We must wait until it is time."

At first you seemed to be very much surprised. And then you laughed to yourself. You said to me :

" I am always thinking that I am at home !"

Just so. Everybody knows that when it is noon in the United States the sun is setting over France. If you could fly to France in one minute, you could go straight into the sunset, right from noon. Unfortunately, France is too far away for that. But on your tiny planet, my little prince, all you need do is move your chair a few steps. You can see the day end and the twilight falling whenever you like...

" One day," you said to me, " I saw the sunset forty-four times !"

And a little later you added :

" You know—one loves the sunset, when one is so sad..."

" Were you so sad, then ?" I asked, " on the day of the

forty-four sunsets ?"

But the little prince made no reply.

7

On the fifth day—again, as always, it was thanks to the sheep
—the secret of the little prince's life was revealed to me.

Abruptly, without anything to lead up to it, and as if the question had been born of long and silent meditation on his problem, he demanded :

" A sheep—if it eats little bushes, does it eat flowers, too ?"

" A sheep," I answered, " eats anything it finds in its reach."

" Even flowers that have thorns?"

" Yes, even flowers that have thorns."

" Then the thorns—what use are they ?"

I did not know. At that moment I was very busy trying to unscrew a bolt that had got stuck in my engine. I was very much worried, for it was becoming clear to me that the breakdown of my plane was extremely serious. And I had so little drinking water left that I had to fear the worst.

" The thorns—what use are they ?"

The little prince never let go of a question, once he had asked it. As for me, I was upset over that bolt. And I answered with the first thing that came into my head :

" The thorns are of no use at all. Flowers have thorns just for spite !"

" Oh !"

There was a moment of complete silence. Then the little prince flashed back at me, with a kind of resentfulness :

" I don't believe you ! Flowers are weak creatures. They are naïve. They reassure themselves as best they can. They believe that their thorns are terrible weapons..."

I did not answer. At that instant I was saying to myself : " If this bolt still won't turn, I am going to knock it out with the hammer." Again the little prince disturbed my thoughts :

" And you actually believe that the flowers—"

" Oh, no !" I cried.   " No, no, no ! I don't believe anything. I answered you with the first thing that came into my head. Don't you see—I am very busy with matters of consequence !"

He stared at me, thunderstruck.

"   Matters   of consequence!"

He looked at me there, with my hammer in my hand, my fingers black with engine-grease, bending down over an object which seemed to him extremely ugly...

" You talk just like the grown-ups !"

That made me a little ashamed. But he went on, relentlessly :

" You mix everything up together.   You confuse everything..."

He was really very angry. He tossed his golden curls in the breeze.

" I know a planet where there is a certain red-faced gentleman. He has never smelled a flower. He has never looked at a star. He has never loved any one. He has never done anything in his life but add up figures. And all day he says over and over, just like you : ' I am busy with matters of consequence !' And that makes him swell up with pride. But he is not a man — he is a mushroom !"

" A what ?"

" A mushroom !"

The little prince was now white with rage.

" The flowers have been growing thorns for millions of years. For millions of years the sheep have been eating them just the same. And is it not a matter of consequence to try to understand why the flowers go to so much trouble to grow thorns which are never of any use to them? Is the warfare between the sheep and the flowers not important ? Is this not of more consequence than a fat red-faced gentleman's sums ? And if I know—I, myself—one flower which is unique in the world, which grows nowhere but on my planet, but which one little sheep can destroy in a single bite some morning, without even noticing what he is doing—Oh ! You think that is not important !"

His face turned from white to red as he continued :

" If some one loves a flower, of which just one single blossom grows in all the millions and millions of stats, it is enough to make him happy just to look at the stats. He can say to himself : 'Somewhere, my flower is there...' But if the sheep eats the flower, in one moment all his stars will be darkened...And you think that is not important !"

He could not say anything more. His words were choked by sobbing.

The night had fallen. I had let my tools drop from my hands. Of what moment now was my hammer, my bolt, or thirst, or death ? On one star, one planet, my planet, the Earth, there was a little prince to be comforted. I took him in my arms, and rocked him. I said to him :

" The flower that you love is not in danger. I will draw you a muzzle for your sheep. I will draw you a railing to put around your flower. I will—"

I did not know what to say to him. I felt awkward and blundering. I did not know how I could reach him, where I could overtake him and go on hand in hand with him once more.

It is such a secret place, the land of tears.

I soon learned to know this flower better. On the little prince's planet the flowers had always been very simple. They had only one ring of petals ; they took up no room at all ; they were a trouble to nobody. One morning they would appear in the grass, and by night they would have faded peacefully away. But one day, from a seed blown from no one knew where, a new flower had come up ; and the little prince had watched very closely over this small sprout which was not like any other small sprouts on his planet. It might, you see, have been a new kind of baobab.

But the shrub soon stopped growing, and began to get ready to produce a flower. The little prince, who was present at the first appearance of a huge bud, felt at once that some sort of miraculous apparition must emerge from it. But the flower was not satisfied to complete the preparations for her beauty in the shelter of her green chamber. She chose her colours with the greatest care. She dressed herself slowly. She adjusted her petals one by one. She did not wish to go out into the world all rumpled, like the field poppies. It was only in the full radiance of her beauty that she wished to appear. Oh, yes! She was a coquettish creature! And her mysterious adornment lasted for days and days.

Then one morning, exactly at sunrise, she suddenly showed herself.

And, after working with all this painstaking precision, she yawned and said :

" Ah! I am scarcely awake. I beg that you will excuse me. My petals are still all disarranged..."

But the little prince could not restrain his admiration :

" Oh! How beautiful you are!"

" Am I not ?" the flower responded, sweetly. "And I was born at the same moment as the sun..."

The little prince could guess easily enough that she was not any too modest—but how moving

—and exciting—she was!

" I think it is time for breakfast," she added an instant later. " If you would have the kindness to think of my needs—"

And the little prince, completely abashed, went to look for a sprinkling-can of fresh water. So, he tended the flower.

So, too, she began very quickly to torment him with her vanity—which was, if the truth be known, a little difficult to deal with. One day, for instance, when she was speaking of her four thorns, she said to the little prince :

" Let the tigers come with their claws!"

" There are no tigers on my planet," the little prince objected.

" And, anyway, tigers do not eat weeds."

" I am not a weed," the flower replied, sweetly.

" Please excuse me..."

" I am not at all afraid of tigers," she went on, "but I have a horror of draughts. I suppose you wouldn't have a screen for me?"

"A horror of draughts—that is bad luck, for a plant," remarked the little prince, and added to himself, "This flower is a very complex creature..."

"At night I want you to put me under a glass globe. It is very cold where you live. In the place where I came from—"

But she interrupted herself at that point. She had come in the form of a seed. She could not have known anything of any other worlds. Embarrassed over having let herself be caught on the verge of such a naïve untruth, she coughed two or three times, in order to put the little prince in th wrong.

" The screen ?"

" I was just going to look for it when you spoke to me..."

Then she forced her cough a little more so that the should suffer from remorse just the same.

So the little prince, in spite of all the good will that was inseparable from his love, had soon come to doubt her. He had taken seriously words which were without importance, and it made him very unhappy.

" I ought not to have listened to her," he confided to me one day.

" One never ought to listen to the flowers. One should simply look at them and breathe their fragrance. Mine perfumed all my planet. But I did not know how to take pleasure in all her grace. This tale of claws, which disturbed me so much, should only have filled my heart with tenderness and pity."

And he continued his confidences:

" The fact is that I did not know how to understand anything! I ought to have judged by deeds and not by words. She cast her fragrance and her radiance over me. I ought never to have run away from her ... I ought to have guessed all the affection that lay behind her poor little stratagems. Flowers are so inconsistent! But I was too young to know how to love her ... "

9

I believe that for his escape he took advantage of the migration of a flock of wild birds. On the morning of his departure he put his planet in perfect order. He carefully cleaned out his active volcanoes. He possessed two active volcanoes; and they were very convenient for heating his breakfast in the morning. He also had one volcano that was extinct. But, as he said, " One never knows!" So he cleaned out the extinct volcano, too. If they are well cleaned out, volcanoes burn slowly and steadily, without any eruptions. Volcanic eruptions are like fires in a chimney.

On our earth we are obviously much too small to clean out our volcanoes. That is why they bring no end of trouble upon us.

The little prince also pulled up, with a certain sense of dejection, the last little shoots of the baobabs. He believed that he would never want to return. But on this last morning all these familiar tasks seemed very precious to him. And when he watered the flower for the last time, and prepared to place her under the shelter of her glass globe, he realized that he was very close to tears.

" Goodbye," he said to the flower.
But she made no answer.
" goodbye," he said again.
The flower coughed. But it was not because she had a cold.

"He carefully cleaned out his active volcanoes."

" I have been silly," she said to him, at last. " I ask your forgiveness. Try to be happy..."

He was surprised by this absence of reproaches. He stood there all bewildered, the glass globe held arrested in midair. He did not understand this quiet sweetness.

" Of course I love you," the flower said to him. " it is my fault that you have not known it all the while. That is of no importance. But you—you have been just as foolish as I. Try to be happy...Let the glass globe be. I don't want it any more."

" But the wind—"

" My cold is not so bad as all that...The cool night air will do me good. I am a flower."

" But the animals—"

" Well, I must endure the presence of two or three caterpillars if I wish to become acquainted with the butterflies. It seems that they are very beautiful. And if not the butterflies —and the caterpillars—who will call upon me? You will be far away...As for the large animals—I am not at all afraid of any of them. I have my claws."

And, naïvely, she showed her four thorns. Then she added :

" Don't linger like this. You have decided to go away. Now go!"

For she did not want him to see her crying. She was such a proud flower...

10

He found himself in the neighbourhood of the asteroids 325,

326, 327, 328, 329, and 330. He began, therefore, by visiting them, in order to add to his knowledge.

The first of them was inhabited by a king. Clad in royal purple and ermine, he was seated upon a throne which was at the same time both simple and majestic.

" Ah ! Here is a subject," exclaimed the king, when he saw the little prince coming.

And the little prince asked himself :

" How could he recognize me when he had never seen me

before ?"

He did not know how the world is simplified for kings. To them, all men are subjects.

" Approach, so that I may see you better," said the king, who felt consumingly proud of being at last a king over somebody.

The little prince looked everywhere to find a place to sit down ; but the entire planet was crammed and obstructed by the king's magnificent ermine robe. So he remained standing upright, and, since he was tired, he yawned.

" It is contrary to etiquette to yawn in the presence of a king," the monarch said to him. " I forbid you to do so."

" I can't help it. I can't stop myself," replied the little prince, thoroughly embarrassed. " I have come on a long journey, and I have had no sleep..." "Ah, then, " the king said. " I order you to yawn. It is years since I have seen anyone yawning. Yawns, to me, are objects of curiosity. Come, now ! Yawn again ! It is an order."

" That frightens me ... I cannot, any more ..."

Murmured the little prince, now completely abashed.

" Hum ! Hum !" replied the king. " Then I—I order you sometimes to yawn and sometimes to—"

He spluttered a little, and seemed vexed,

For what the king fundamentally insisted upon was that his authority should be respected. He tolerated no disobedience. He was an absolute monarch. But, because he was a very good man, he made his orders reasonable.

" If I ordered a general," he would say, by way of example, " if I ordered a general to change himself into a sea bird, and if the general did not obey me, that would not be the fault of the general. It would be my fault."

" May I sit down ?" came now a timid inquiry from the little prince.

" I order you to do so," the king answered him, and majestically gathered in a fold of his ermine mantle.

But the little prince was wondering ... The planet was tiny. Over what could this king really rule?

" Sire," he said to him, " I beg that you will excuse my asking you a question—"

" I order you to ask me a question," the king hastened to assure him.

" Sire—over what do you rule?"

" Over everything," said the king, with magnificent simplicity.

" Over everything?"

The king made a gesture, which took in his planet, the other planets, and all the stars.

" Over all that?" asked the little prince.

"Over all that," the king answered.

For his rule was not only absolute : It was also universal.

" And the stars obey you?"

" Certainly they do," the king said. " They obey instantly. I do not permit insubordination."

Such power was a thing for the little prince to marvel at. If he had been master of such complete authority, he would have been able to watch the sunset, not forty-four times in one day, but seventy-two, or even a hundred, or even two hundred times, without ever having to move his chair. And because he felt a bit sad as he remembered his little planet which he had forsaken, he plucked up his courage to ask the king a favour :

" I should like to see a sunset ... Do me that kindness ... Order the sun to set ... "

" If I ordered a general to fly from one flower to another like a butterfly, or to write a tragic drama, or to change himself into a sea bird, and if the general did not carry out the order that he had received, which one of us would be in the wrong?" the king demanded " The general, or myself?"

" You," said the prince firmly.

" Exactly. One must require from each one the duty which each one can perform," the king went on. " Accepted authority rests first of all on reason. If you ordered your people to go and throw themselves into the sea, they would rise up in revolution. I have the right to require obedience because my orders are reasonable."

" Then my sunset?" the little prince reminded him : for he never forgot a question once he had asked it.

" You shall have your sunset. I shall command it. But, according to my science of government, I shall wait until conditions are favourable."

" When will that be?" inquired the little prince.

" Hum ! Hum !" replied the king ; and before saying anything else he consulted a bulky almanac. " Hum ! Hum ! That will be about—about—that will be this evening about twenty minutes to eight. And you will see how well I am obeyed !"

The little prince yawned. He was regretting his lost sunset.

And then, too, he was already beginning to be a little bored.

" I have nothing more to do here," he said to the king. " So I shall set out on my way again."

" Do not go," said the king, who was very proud of having a subject. " Do not go. I will make you a Minister !"

" Minister of what ?"

" Minister of—of Justice !"

" But there is nobody here to judge !"

" We do not know that," the king said to him. " I have not yet made a complete tour of my kingdom. I am very old. There is no room here for a carriage. And it tires me to walk."

" Oh, but I have looked already !" said the little prince, turning around to give one more glance to the other side of the planet. On that side, as on this, there was nobody at all ...

" Then you shall judge yourself," the king answered. "That is the most difficult thing of all. It is much more difficult to judge oneself than to judge others. If you succeed in judging yourself rightly, then you are indeed a man of true wisdom."

" Yes," said the little prince, " but I can judge myself anywhere. I do not need to live on this planet."

" Hum ! Hum !" said the king. " I have good reason to believe that somewhere on my planet there is an old rat. I hear him at night. You can judge this old rat. From time to time you will condemn him to death. Thus his life will depend on your justice. But you will pardon him on each occasion ; for he must be treated thriftily. He is the only one we have."

"I," replied the little prince, " do not like to condemn anyone to death. And now I think I will go on my way."

" No," said the king.

But the little prince, having now completed his preparations for departure, had no wish to grieve the old monarch.

" If your Majesty wishes to be promptly obeyed," he said, " he should be able to give me a reasonable order."

He should be able, for example, to order me to be gone by the end of one minute. It seems to me that conditions are favourable ...

As the king made no answer, the little prince hesitated a moment. Then, with a sigh, he took his leave.

" I make you my Ambassador," the king called out, hastily.

He had a magnificent air of authority.

" The grown-ups are very strange," the little prince said to himself, as he continued on his journey.

11

The second planet was inhabited by a conceited man.

" Ah ! Ah ! I am about to receive a visit from an admirer !" he exclaimed, from afar, when he first saw the little prince coming.

For, to conceited men, all other men are admirers.

" Good morning," said the little prince. " That is a queer hat you are wearing."

" It is a hat for salutes," the conceited man replied. " It is to raise in salute when people acclaim me. Unfortunately, nobody at all ever passes this way."

" Yes ?" said the little prince, who did not understand what the conceited man was talking about.

" Clap your hands, one against the other," the conceited man now directed him.

The little prince clapped his hands. The conceited man raised his hat in a modest salute.

" This is more entertaining than the visit to the king," the little prince said to himself. And he began again to clap his hands, one against the other. The conceited man again raised his hat in salute.

After five minutes of this exercise the little prince grew tired of the game's monotony.

" And what should one do to make the hat come down ?" he asked.

But the conceited man did not hear him. Conceited people never hear anything but praise.

" Do you really admire me very much ?" he demanded of the little prince.

" What does that mean— 'admire' ?"

" To admire means that you regard me as the handsomest, the best-dressed, the richest, and the most intelligent man on this planet."

" But you are the only man on your planet !"

" Do me this kindness. Admire me just the same."

" I admire you," said the little prince, shrugging his shoulders slightly, " but what is there in that to interest you so much ?"

And the little prince went away.

" The grown-ups are certainly very odd," he said to himself, as he continued on his journey.

12

The next planet was inhabited by a tippler. This was a very short visit, but it plunged the little prince into deep dejection.

" What are you doing there?" he said to the tippler, whom he found settled down in silence before a collection of empty bottles and also a collection of full bottles.

" I am drinking," replied the tippler, with a lugubrious air.

" Why are you drinking ?" demanded the little prince.

" So that I may forget," replied the tippler.

" Forget what ?" inquired the little prince, who already was sorry for him.

" Forget that I am ashamed," the tippler confessed, hanging his head.

" Ashamed of what ?" insisted the little prince, who wanted to help him.

" Ashamed of drinking !" The tippler brought his speech to an end, and shut himself up in an impregnable silence.

And the little prince went away, puzzled.

" The grown-ups are certainly very, very odd," he said to himself, as he continued on his journey.

13.

The fourth planet belonged to a businessman. This man was so much occupied that he did not even raise his head at the little prince's arrival.

"Good morning," the little prince said to him. "Your cigarette has gone out."

"Three and two make five. Five and seven make twelve. Twelve and three make fifteen. Good morning. Fifteen and seven make twenty-two. Twenty-two and six make twenty-eight. I haven't time to light it again. Twenty-six and five make thirty-one. Phew! Then that makes five-hundred-and-one million, six-hundred-twenty-two thousand, seven-hundred-thirty-one."

" Five hundred million what ?" asked the little prince.

" Eh ? Are you still there? Five-hundred-and-one million—I can't stop ... I have so much to do ! I am concerned with matters of consequence. I don't amuse myself with balderdash. Two and five make seven ..."

" Five-hundred-and-one million what?" repeated the little prince, who never in his life had let go of a question once he had asked it.

The businessman raised his head.

" During the fifty-four years that I have inhabited this planet, I have been disturbed only three times. The first time was twenty-two years ago, when some giddy goose fell from goodness knows where. He make the most frightful noise that resounded all over the place, and I made four mistakes in my addition. The second time, eleven years ago, I was disturbed by an attack of rheumatism. I don't get enough exercise. I have no time for loafing. The third time—well, this is it ! I was saying, then, five-hundred-and-one millions—"

" Millions of what ?"

The businessman suddenly realized that there was no hope of being left in peace until he answered this question.

" Millions of those little objects," he said, " which one sometimes sees in the sky."

" Flies ?"

" Oh, no. Little glittering objects."

" Bees ?"

" Oh, no. Little golden objects that set lazy men to idle dreaming. As for me, I am concerned with matters of consequence. There is no time for idle dreaming in my life."

" Ah ! You mean the stars ?"

" Yes, that's it. The stars."

" And what do you do with five-hundred millions of stars ?"

" Five-hundred-and-one million, six-hundred-twenty-two thousand, seven-hundred-thirty-one. I am concerned with matters of consequence : I am accurate."

" And what do you do with these stars ?"

" What do I do with them ?"

" Yes."

" Nothing. I own them."

" You own the stars ?"

" Yes."

" But I have already seen a king who—"

" Kings do not *own*, they *reign over*. It is a very different matter."

" And what good does it do you to own the stars ?"

" It does me the good of making me rich."

" And what good does it do you to be rich ?"

" It makes it possible for me to buy more stars, if any are discovered."

" This man," the little Prince said to himself, " reasons like my poor tippler ... "

Nevertheless, he still had some more questions.

" How is it possible for one to own the stars ?"

" To whom do they belong ?" the businessman retorted, peevishly.

" I don't know. To nobody."

" Then they belong to me, because I was the first person to think of it."

" Is that all that is necessary ?"

" Certainly. When you find a diamond that belongs to nobody, it is yours. When you discover an island that belongs to nobody, it is yours. When you get an idea before any one else, you take out a patent on it : it is yours. So with me : I own the stars, because nobody else before me ever thought of owning them."

" Yes, that is true," said the little prince. " And what do you do with them ?"

" I administer them," replied the businessman. " I count them and recount them. It is difficult. But I am a man who is naturally interested in matters of consequence."

The little prince was still not satisfied.

" If I owned a silk scarf," he said, " I could put it around my neck and take it away with me. If I owned a flower, I could pluck that flower and take it away with me. But you cannot pluck the stars from heaven ..."

" No. But I can put them in the bank."

" Whatever does that mean ?"

" That means that I write the number of my stars on a little paper. And then I put his paper in a drawer and lock it with a key."

" And that is all ?"

" That is enough," said the businessman.

" It is entertaining," thought the little prince. " It is rather poetic. But it is of no great consequence."

On matters of consequence, the little prince had ideas which were very different from those of the grown-ups.

" I myself own a flower," he continued his conversation

with the businessman, "which I water every day. I own three volcanoes, which I clean out every week (for I also clean out the one that is extinct ; one never knows). It is of some use to my volcanoes, and it is of some use to my flower, that I own them. But you are of no use to the stars ... "

The businessman opened his mouth, but he found nothing to say in answer. And the little prince went away.

"The grown-ups are certainly altogether extraordinary," he said simply, talking to himself as he continued on his journey.

14.

The fifth planet was very strange. It was the smallest of all. There was just enough room on it for a street lamp and a lamplighter. The little prince was not able to reach any explanation of the use of a street lamp and a lamplighter, somewhere in the heavens, on a planet which was so small that it had no people, and not one house. But he said to himself, nevertheless: "It may well be that this man is absurd. But he is not so absurd as the king, the conceited man, the businessman, and the tippler. For at least his work has some meaning. When he lights his street lamp, it is as if he brought one more star to life, or one flower. When he puts out his lamp, he sends the flower, or the star, to sleep. That is a beautiful occupation. And since it is beautiful, it is truly useful."

When he arrived on the planet he respectfully saluted the lamplighter.

"Good morning, sir. Why have you just put out your lamp?

"I follow a terrible profession."

"

"Those are the orders," replied the lamplighter. "Good morning."

"What are the orders ?"

"The orders are that I put out my lamp. Good evening."

And he lighted his lamp again.

"But why have you just lighted it again ?"

"Those are the orders," replied the lamplighter.

"I do not understand," said the little prince.

"There is nothing to understand," said the lamplighter. "Orders are orders. Good morning."

And he put out his lamp.

Then he mopped his forehead with a handkerchief decorated with red squares.

"I follow a terrible profession. In the old days it was reasonable. I put the lamp out in the morning, and in the evening I lighted it again. I had the rest of the day for relaxation and the rest of the night for sleep."

"And the orders have been changed since that time ?"

"The orders have not been changed," said the lamplighter. "That is the tragedy to me ! From year to year the planet has turned more rapidly and the orders have not been changed !"

"Then what ?" asked the little prince.

"Then—the planet now makes a complete turn every minute, and I no longer have a single second for repose. Once every minute I have to light my lamp and put it out !"

"That is very funny ! A day lasts only one minute, here where you live !"

"It is not funny at all !" said the lamplighter. "While we

have been talking together a month has gone by."

" A month ?"

" Yes, a month. Thirty minutes. Thirty days. Good evening."

And he lighted his lamp again.

As the little prince watched him, he felt that he loved this lamplighter who was so faithful to his orders. He remembered the sunsets which he himself had gone to seek, in other days, merely by pulling up his chair ; and he wanted to help his friend.

" You know," he said, " I can tell you a way you can rest whenever you want to ..."

" I always wan to rest," said the lamplighter.

For it is possible for a man to be faithful and lazy at the same time.

The little prince went on with his explanation :

" Your planet is so small that three strides will take you all the way around it. To be always in the sunshine, you need only walk along rather slowly. When you want to rest, you will walk —and the day will last as long as you like."

" That doesn't do me much good," said the lamplighter. " The one thing I love in life is to sleep."

" Then you're unlucky," said the little prince.

" I am unlucky," said the lamplighter. " Good morning."

And he put out his lamp.

" That man," said the little prince to himself, as he continued farther on his journey, " that man would be scorned by all the others : by the king, by the conceited man, by the tippler, by the businessman. Nevertheless he is the only one of them all who does not seem to me ridiculous. Perhaps that is because he is thinking of something else besides himself."

He breathed a sigh of regret, and said to himself again :

" That man is the only one of them all whom I could have made my friend. But his planet is indeed too small. There is no room on it for two people ..."

What the little prince did not dare confess was that he was sorry most of all to leave this planet, because it was blest every day with 1440 sunsets !

15

The sixth planet was ten times larger than the last one. It was inhabited by an old gentleman who wrote voluminous books.

" Oh, look ! Here is an explorer !" he exclaimed to himself when he saw the little prince coming.

The little prince sat down on the table and panted a little. He had already travelled so much and so far !

" Where do you come from ?" the old gentleman said to him.

" What is that big book ?" said the little prince. " What are you doing ?"

" I am a geographer," said the old gentleman.

" What is a geographer," asked the little prince.

" A geographer is a scholar who knows the location of all the seas, rivers, towns, mountains, and deserts."

" That is very interesting," said the little prince. " Here at last is a man who has a real profession !" And he cast a look around him at the planet of the geographer. It was the most magnificent and stately planet that he had ever seen.

" Your planet is very beautiful," he said. " Has it any mountains ?"

" I couldn't tell you," said the geographer.

" Ah !" The little prince was disappointed. " Has it any oceans ? "

" I couldn't tell you," said the geographer.

" And towns, and rivers and deserts ?"

" I couldn't tell you that, either."

" But you are a geographer !"

" Exactly," the geographer said. " But I am not an explorer. I haven't a single explorer on my planet. It is not the geographer who goes out to count the towns, the rivers, the mountains, the seas, the oceans, and the deserts. The geographer is much too important to go loafing about. He does not leave his desk. But he receives the explorers in his study. He asks them questions, and he notes down what they recall of their travels. And if the recollections of any one among them seem interesting to him, the geographer orders an inquiry into that explorer's moral character."

" Why is that ?"

" Because an explorer who told lies would bring disaster on the books of the geographer. So would an explorer who drank too much."

" Why is that?"   asked the little prince.

" Because intoxicated men see double. Then the geographer would note down two mountains in a place where there was only one."

" I know some one,"   said the little prince,   " who would make a bad explorer."

" That is possible. Then, when the moral character of the explorer is shown to be good, an inquiry is ordered into his discovery."

" One goes to see it ?"

" No that would be too complicated. But one requires the explorer to furnish proofs. For example, if the discovery in question is that of a large mountain, one requires that large stones be brought back from it."

The geographer was suddenly stirred to excitement.

" But you—you come from far away ! You are an explorer ! You shall describe your planet to me !"

And, having opened his big register, the geographer sharpened his pencil. The recitals of explorers are put down first in pencil. One waits until the explorer has furnished proofs, before putting them down in ink.

" Well ?" said the geographer expectantly.

" Oh, where I live," said the little prince, " it is not very interesting. It is all so small. I have three volcanoes. Two volcanoes are active and the other is extinct. But one never knows."

" One never knows," said the geographer.

" I have also a flower."

" We do not record flowers," said the geographer.

" Why is that ? The flower is the most beautiful thing on my planet !"

" We do not record them," said the geographer, "because they are ephemeral."

" What does that mean— 'ephemeral' ?"

" Geographies," said the geographer, " are the books which, of all books, are most concerned with matters of consequence. They never become old-fashioned. It is very rarely that a mountain changes its position. It is very rarely that an ocean empties itself of its waters. We write of eternal things."

" But extinct volcanoes may come to life again," that little prince interrupted. "What does that mean— 'ephemeral' ?"

" Whether volcanoes are extinct or alive, it comes to the same thing for us," said the geographer. "The thing that matters to us is the mountain. It does not change."

" But what does that mean— 'ephemeral' ?" repeated the little prince, who never in his life had let go of a question, once he had asked it.

" It means, ' which is in danger of speedy disappearance.' "

" Is my flower in danger of speedy disappearance ?"

" Certainly it is."

" My flower is ephemeral," the little prince said to himself, " and she has only four thorns to defend herself against the world. And I have left her on my planet, all alone !"

That was his first moment of regret. But he took courage once more.

" What place would you advise me to visit now ?" he asked.

" The planet Earth," replied the geographer. " It has a good reputation."

And the little prince went away, thinking of his flower.

16

So then the seventh planet was the Earth.

The Earth is not just an ordinary planet ! One can count, there, 111 kings (not forgetting, to be sure, the Negro kings among them), 7,000 geographers, 900,000 businessmen, 7,500,000 tipplers, 311,000,000 conceited men—that is to say, about 2,000,000,000 grow-ups.

To give you an idea of the size of the Earth, I will tell you that before the invention of electricity it was necessary to maintain, over the whole of the six continents, a veritable army of 462,511 lamplighters for the street lamps.

Seen from a slight distance, that would make a splendid spectacle. The movements of this army would be regulated like those of the ballet in the opera. First would come the turn of the lamplighters of New Zealand and Australia. Having set their lamps alight, these would go off to sleep. Next, the lamplighters of China and Siberia would enter for their steps in the dance, and then they too would be waved back into the wings. After that would come the turn of the lamplighters of Russia and the Indies ; then those of Africa and Europe ; then those of South America ; then those of North America. And never would they make a mistake in the order of their entry upon the stage. It would be magnificent.

Only the man who was in charge of the single lamp at the North Pole, and his colleague who was responsible for the single lamp at the South Pole—only these two would live free from toil and care : they would be busy twice a year.

17.

When one wishes to play the wit, he sometimes wanders a little from the truth. I have not been altogether honest in what I have told you about the lamplighters. And I realize that I run the risk of giving a false idea of our planet to those who do not know it. Men occupy a very small space upon the Earth. If the two billion inhabitants who people its surface were all to stand upright and somewhat crowded together, as they do for some big public assembly, they could easily be put into one public square twenty miles long and twenty miles wide. All humanity could be piled up on a small Pacific islet.

The grown-ups, to be sure, will not believe you when you tell them that. They imagine that they fill a great deal of space. They fancy themselves as important as the baobabs. You should advise them, then, to make their own calculations. They adore figures, and that will please them. But do not waste your time on this extra task. It is unnecessary. You have, I know,

"You are a funny animal . . . You are no thicker than a finger ."

confidence in me.

When the little prince arrived on the Earth, he was very much surprised not to see any people. He was beginning to be afraid he had come to the wrong planet, when a coil of gold, the colour of the moonlight, flashed across the sand.

" Good evening," said the little prince courteously.

" Good evening," said the snake.

" What planet is this on which I have come down ?" asked the little prince.

" This is the Earth ; this is Africa," the snake answered.

" Ah ! Then there are no people on the Earth ?"

" This is the desert. There are no people in the desert. The Earth is large," said the snake.

The little prince sat down on a stone, and raised his eyes toward the sky.

" I wonder," he said, " whether the stars are set alight in heaven so that one day each one of us may find his own again ... Look at my planet. It is right there above us. But how far away it is !"

" It is beautiful," the snake said. " What has brought you here?"

" I have been having some trouble with a flower," said the little prince.

" Ah !" said the snake.

And they were both silent.

" Where are the men ?" the little prince at last took up the conversation again. " It is a little lonely in the desert ..."

" It is also lonely among men," the snake said.

The little prince gazed at him for a long time.

" You are a funny animal," he said at last. " You are no thicker than a finger ..."

" But I am more powerful than the finger of a king," said the snake.

The little prince smiled.

" You are not very powerful. You haven't even any feet. You cannot even travel ..."

" I can carry you farther than any ship could take you," said the snake.

He twined himself around the little prince's ankle, like a golden bracelet.

" Whomever I touch, I send back to the earth from whence they came," the snake spoke again. " But you are innocent and true, and you come from a star ..."

The little prince made no reply.

" You move me to pity—you are so weak on this Earth made of granite," the snake said. " I can help you, some day, if you grow too homesick for your own planet. I can—"

" Oh ! I understand you very well," said the little prince. " But why do you always speak in riddles ?"

" I solve them all," said the snake.

And they were both silent.

18

The little prince crossed the desert and met with only one flower. It was a flower with three petals, a flower of no account at all.

" Good morning," said the little prince.

" Good morning," said the flower.

" Where are the men ?" the little prince asked, politely.

The flower had once seen a caravan passing.

" Men ?" she echoed. " I think there are six or seven of them in existence. I saw them, several years ago. But one never knows where to find them. The wind blows them away. They have no roots, and that makes their life very difficult."

" Goodbye," said the little prince.

" Goodbye," said the flower.

19

After that, the little prince climbed a high mountain. The only mountains he had ever known were the three volcanoes, which came up to his knees. And he used the extinct volcano as a foot-stool. " From a mountain as high as this one," he said to himself, " I shall be able to see the whole planet at one glance, and all the people ..."

But he saw nothing, save peaks of rock that were sharpened like needles.

" Good morning," he said courteously.

" Good morning—Good morning—Good morning," answered the echo.

" Who are you ?" said the little Prince.

" Who are you—Who are you—Who are you ?" answered the echo.

" Be my friends. I am all alone," he said.

" I am all alone—all alone—all alone," answered the echo.

" What a queer planet !" he thought. " It is altogether dry, and altogether pointed, and altogether harsh and forbidding. And the people have no imagination. They repeat whatever one says to them ... On my planet I had a flower; she always was the first to speak ..."

"This planet is altogether dry, and altogether pointed."

20

But it happened that after walking for a long time through sand, and rocks, and snow, the little prince at last came upon a road. And all roads lead to the abodes of men.

"Good morning," he said.

He was standing before a garden, all a-bloom with roses.

"Good morning," said the roses.

The little prince gazed at them. They all looked like his flower.

"Who are you?" he demanded, thunderstruck.

"We are roses," the roses said.

And he was overcome with sadness. His flower had told him that she was the only one of her kind in all the universe. And here were five thousand of them, all alike, in one single garden !

"She would be very much annoyed," he said to himself, "if she could see that ... She would cough most dreadfully, and she would pretend that she was dying, to avoid being laughed at. And I should be obliged to pretend that I was nursing her back to life—for if I did not do that, to humble myself also, she would really allow herself to die ..."

Then he went on with his reflections : "I thought that I was rich, with a flower that was unique in all the world ; and all I had was a common rose. A common rose, and three volcanoes that come up to my knees—and one of them perhaps extinct forever ... That doesn't make me a very great prince ..."

And he lay down in the grass and cried.

"And he lay down in the grass and cried."

21

It was then that the fox appeared.

"Good morning," said the fox.

"Good morning," the little prince responded politely, although when he turned around he saw nothing.

"I am right here," the voice said, "under the apple tree."

"Who are you ?" asked the little prince, and added, "You are very pretty to look at."

"I am a fox," the fox said.

"Come and play with me," proposed the little prince. "I am so unhappy."

"I cannot play with you," the fox said. "I am not tamed."

"Ah ! Please excuse me," said the little prince.

But, after some thought, he added :

"What does that mean— 'tame' ?"

"You do not live here," said the fox. "What is it that you are looking for ?"

"I am looking for men," said the little prince. "What does that mean — 'tame' ?"

"Men," said the fox. "They have guns, and they hunt.

It is very disturbing. They also raise chickens. These are their only interests. Are you looking for chickens ?"

"No," said the little prince. "I am looking for friends. What does that mean— 'tame' ?"

"It is an act too often neglected," said the fox. "It means to establish ties."

" 'To establish ties' ?"

" Just that," said the fox. " To me, you are still nothing more than a little boy who is just like a hundred thousand other little boys. And I have no need of you. And you, on your part, have no need of me. To you, I am nothing more than a fox like a hundred thousand other foxes. But if you tame me, then we shall need each other. To me, you will be unique in all the world. To you, I shall be unique in all the world ..."

" I am beginning to understand," said the little prince. " There is a flower ... I think that she has tamed me ..."

" It is possible," said the fox. " On the Earth one sees all sorts of things."

" Oh, but this is not on the Earth !" said the little prince.

The fox seemed perplexed, and very curious.

" On another planet ?"

" Yes."

" Are there hunters on that planet ?"

" No."

" Ah, that is interesting ! Are there chickens ?"

" No."

" Nothing is perfect," sighed the fox.

But he came back to his idea.

" My life is very monotonous," he said. " I hunt chickens ; men hunt me. All the chickens are just alike, and all men are just alike. And, in consequence, I am a little bored. But if you tame me, it will be as if the sun came to shine on my life. I shall know the sound of a step that will be different from all the others. Other steps send me hurrying back underneath the ground. Yours will call me, like music, out of my burrow. And then look : you see the grain-fields down yonder ? I do not eat bread. Wheat is of no use to me. The wheat fields have nothing to say to me. And that is sad. But you have hair that is the colour of gold. Think how wonderful that will be when you have tamed me ! The grain, which is also golden, will bring me back the thought of you. And I shall love to listen to the wind in the wheat ..."

The fox gazed at the little prince, for a long time.

" Please—tame me !" he said.

" I want to, very much," the little prince replied. " But I have not much time. I have friends to discover, and a great many things to understand."

" One only understands the things that one tames," said the fox. " Men have no more time to understand anything. They buy things all ready made at the shops. But there is no shop anywhere where one can buy friendship, and so men have no friends any more. If you want a friend, tame me ..."

" What must I do, to tame you ?" asked the little prince.

" You must be very patient," replied the fox. " First you will sit down at a little distance from me—like that—in the grass. I shall look at you out of the corner of my eye, and you will say nothing. Words are the source of misunderstandings. But you will sit a little closer to me, every day ..."

The next day the little prince came back.

" It would have been better to come back at the same hour," said the fox. " If, for example, you came at four o'clock in the afternoon, then at three o'clock I shall begin to be happy. I shall feel happier and happier as the hour advances. At four o' clock, I shall already be worrying and jumping about. I shall show you how happy I am ! But if you come at just any time, I shall never know at what hour my heart is to be ready to greet you ... One must observe the proper rites ..."

" What is a rite ?" asked the little prince.

" Those also are actions too often neglected," said the fox. " They are what make one day different from other days, one hour from other hours. There is a rite, for example, among my hunters. Every Thursday they dance with the village girls. So

Thursday is a wonderful day for me ! I can take a walk as far as the vineyards. But if the hunters danced at just any time, every day would be like every other day, and I should never have any vacation at all."

So the little prince tamed the fox. And when the hour of his departure drew near—

" Ah," said the fox, " I shall cry."

" It is your own fault," said the little prince. " I never wished you any sort of harm ; but you wanted me to tame you ..."

" Yes, that is so," said the fox.

"But now you are going to cry!" said the little prince.

"Yes, that is so," said the fox.

" Then it has done you no good at all !"

" It has done me good," said the fox, " because of the colour of the wheat fields." And then he added :

" Go and look again at the roses. You will understand now that yours is unique in all the world. Then come back to say goodbye to me, and I will make you a present of a secret."

The little prince went away, to look again at the roses.

"If you come at four o'clock in the afternoon, then by three o'clock I shall begin to be happy."

" You are not at all like my rose," he said. " As yet you are nothing. No one has tamed you, and you have tamed no one. You are like my fox when I first knew him. He was only a fox like a hundred thousand other foxes. But I have made him my friend, and now he is unique in all the world."

And the roses were very much embarrassed.

" You are beautiful, but you are empty," he went on. " One could not die for you. To be sure, an ordinary passer-by would think that my rose looked just like you—the rose that belongs to me. But in herself alone she is more important than all the hundreds of you other roses : because it is she that I have watered ; because it is she that I have put under the glass globe ; because it is she that I have sheltered behind the screen ; because it is for her that I have killed the caterpillars (except the two or three that we saved to become butterflies) ; because it is she that I have listened to, when she grumbled, or boasted, or even sometimes when she said nothing. Because she is *my* rose."

And he went back to meet the fox.

" Goodbye," he said.

" Goodbye," said the fox. " And now here is my secret, a very simple secret : It is only with the heart that one can see rightly ; what is essential is invisible to the eye."

" What is essential is invisible to the eye," the little prince repeated, so that he would be sure to remember.

" It is the time you have wasted for your rose that makes your rose so important."

" It is the time I have wasted for my rose—" said the little prince, so that he would be sure to remember.

" Men have forgotten this truth," said the fox. " But you must not forget it. You become responsible, forever, for what you have tamed. You are responsible for your rose ..."

" I am responsible for my rose," the little prince repeated, so that he would be sure to remember.

22

" Good morning," said the little prince.

" Good morning," said the railway switchman.

" What do you do here ?" the little prince asked.

" I sort out travelers, in bundles of a thousand," said the switchman. " I send off the trains that carry them : now to the right, now to the left."

And a brilliantly lighted express train shook the switchman's cabin as it rushed by with a roar like thunder.

" They are in a great hurry," said the little prince. " What are they looking for ?"

" Not even the locomotive engineer knows that," said the switchman.

And a second brilliantly lighted express thundered by, in the opposite direction.

"Are they coming back already ?" demanded the little prince.

" These are not the same ones," said the switchman. " It is an exchange."

" Were they not satisfied where they were ?" asked the little prince.

" No one is ever satisfied where he is," said the switchman.

And they heard the roaring thunder of a third brilliantly lighted express.

" Are they pursuing the first travelers ?" demanded the little prince.

" They are pursuing nothing at all," said the switchman. " They are asleep in there, or if they are not asleep they are yawning. Only the children are flattening their noses against the window-panes."

" Only the children know what they are looking for," said the little prince. " They waste their time over a rag doll and it becomes very important to them ; and if anybody takes it away from them, they cry ..."

" They are lucky," the switchman said.

23

" Good morning," said the little prince.

" Good morning," said the merchant.

This was the merchant who sold pills that had been invented to quench thirst. You need only swallow one pill a week, and you would feel no need of anything to drink.

" Why are you selling those ?" asked the little prince.

" Because they save a tremendous amount of time," said the merchant. " Computations have been made by experts. With these pills, you save fifty-three minutes in every week."

" And what do I do with those fifty-three minutes ?"

" Anything you like ..."

" As for me," said the little prince to himself, " if I had fifty-three minutes to spend as I liked, I should walk at my leisure toward a spring of fresh water."

24.

It was now the eighth day since I had had my accident in the desert, and I had listened to the story of the merchant as I was drinking the last drop of my water supply.

" Ah," I said to the little prince, " these memories of yours are very charming ; but I have not yet succeeded in repairing my plane ; I have nothing more to drink; and I, too, should be very happy if I could walk at my leisure toward a spring of fresh water !"

" My friend the fox—" the little prince said to me.

" My dear little man, this is no longer a matter that has anything to do with the fox !"

" Why not ?"

" Because I am about to die of thirst ..."

He did not follow my reasoning, and he answered me :

" It is a good thing to have a friend, even if one is about to die. I, for instance, am very glad to have a fox as friend ..."

" He has no way of guessing the danger," I said to myself. " He has never been either hungry or thirsty. A little sunshine is all that he needs ..."

But he looked at me steadily, and replied to my thought :

" I am thirsty, too. Let us look for a well ..."

I made a gesture of weariness. It is absurd to look for a well, at random, in the immensity of the desert. But nevertheless we started walking.

When we had trudged along for several hours, in silence, the darkness fell, and the stars began to come out. Thirst had made me a little feverish, and I looked at them as if I were in a dream. The little prince's last words came reeling back into my memory:

" Then you are thirsty, too ?" I demanded.

But he did not reply to my question. He merely said to me :

" Water may also be good for the heart ..."

I did not understand this answer, but I said nothing. I knew very well that it was impossible to cross-examine him.

He was tired. He sat down. I sat down beside him. And,

after a little silence, he spoke again :

" The stars are beautiful, because of a flower that cannot be seen."

I replied, " Yes, that is so." And, without saying anything more, I looked across the ridges of sand that were stretched out before us in the moonlight.

" The desert is beautiful," the little prince added.

And that was true. I have always loved the desert. One sits down on a desert sand dune, sees nothing, hears nothing. Yet through the silence something throbs, and gleams ...

" What makes the desert beautiful," said the little prince, " is that somewhere it hides a well ..."

I was astonished by a sudden understanding of that mysterious radiation of the sands. When I was a little boy I lived in an old house, and legend told us that a treasure was buried there. To be sure, no one had ever known how to find it ; perhaps no one had ever even looked for it. But it cast an enchantment over that house. My home was hiding a secret in the depths of its heart ...

" Yes," I said to the little prince. " The house, the stars, the desert—what gives them their beauty is something that is invisible!"

" I am glad," he said, " that you agree with my fox."

As the little prince dropped off to sleep, I took him in my arms and set out walking once more. I felt deeply moved, and stirred. It seemed to me that I was carrying a very fragile treasure. It seemed to me, even, that there was nothing more fragile on all the Earth. In the moonlight I looked at his pale forehead, his closed eyes, his locks of hair that trembled in the wind, and I said to myself : " What I see here is nothing but a shell. What is most important is invisible ..."

As his lips opened slightly with the suspicion of a half-smile, I said to myself, again : " What moves me so deeply, about this little prince who is sleeping here, is his loyalty to a flower—the image of a rose that shines through his whole being like the flame of a lamp, even when he is asleep ..." And I felt him to be more fragile still. I felt the need of protecting him, as if he himself were a flame that might be extinguished by a little puff of wind ...

And, as I walked on so, I found the well, at daybreak.

25

" Men," said the little prince, " set out on their way in express trains, but they do not know what they are looking for. Then they rush about, and get excited, and turn round and round ..."

And he added :

" It is not worth the trouble ..."

The well that we had come to was not like the wells of the Sahara. The wells of the Sahara are mere holes dug in the sand. This one was like a well in a village. But there was no village here, and I thought I must be dreaming ...

" It is strange," I said to the little prince. " Everything is ready for use : the pulley, the bucket, the rope ..."

He laughed, touched the rope, and set the pulley to working. And the pulley moaned, like an old weathervane which the wind has long since forgotten.

" Do you hear ?" said the little prince. " We have wakened the well, and it is singing ..."

I did not want him to tire himself with the rope.

" Leave it to me," I said. " It is too heavy for you."

I hoisted the bucket slowly to the edge of the well and set it

"He laughed, touched the rope, and set the pulley to working."

there—happy, tired as I was, over my achievement. The song of the pulley was still in my ears, and I could see the sunlight shimmer in the still trembling water.

" I am thirsty for this water," said the little prince. " Give me some of it to drink ... "

And I understood what he had been looking for.

I raised the bucket to his lips. He drank, his eyes closed. It was as sweet as some special festival treat. This water was indeed a different thing from ordinary nourishment. Its sweetness was born of the walk under the stars, the song of the pulley, the effort of my arms. It was good for the heart, like a present. When I was a little boy, the lights of the Christmas tree, the music of the Midnight Mass, the tenderness of smiling faces, used to make up, so, the radiance of the gifts I received.

" The men where you live," said the little prince, " raise five thousand roses in the same garden—and they do not find in it what they are looking for."

" They do not find it," I replied.

" And yet what they are looking for could be found in one single rose, or in a little water."

" Yes, that is true," I said.

And the little prince added :

" But the eyes are blind. One must look with the heart ..."

I had drunk the water. I breathed easily. At sunrise the sand is the colour of honey. And that honey colour was making me happy, too. What brought me, then, this sense of grief ?

" You must keep your promise," said the little prince, softly, as he sat down beside me once more.

" What promise ?"

" You know—a muzzle for my sheep ... I am responsible for this flower ..."

I took my rough drafts of drawings out of my pocket. The little prince looked them over, and laughed as he said :

" Your baobabs—they look a little like cabbages."

" Oh !"

I had been so proud of my baobabs !

" Your fox—his ears look a little like horns ; and they are too long."

And he laughed again.

" You are not fair, little prince," I said. " I don't know how to draw anything except boa constrictors from the outside and boa constrictors from the inside."

" Oh, that will be all right," he said, " children understand."

So then I made a pencil sketch of a muzzle. And as I gave it to him my heart was torn.

" You have plans that I do not know about," I said.

But he did not answer me. He said to me, instead :

" You know—my descent to the earth ... Tomorrow will be its anniversary."

Then, after a silence, he went on :

" I came down very near here."

And he flushed.

And once again, without understanding why, I had a queer sense of sorrow. One question, however, occurred to me :

" Then it was not by chance that on the morning when I first met you—a week ago—you were strolling along like that, all alone, a thousand miles from any inhabited region ? You were on your way back to the place where you landed ?"

The little prince flushed again.

And I added, with some hesitancy :

"Perhaps it was because of the anniversary ?"

The little prince flushed once more. He never answered questions—but when one flushes does that not mean "Yes" ?

"Ah," I said to him, "I am a little frightened—"

But he interrupted me.

"Now you must work. You must return to your engine. I will be waiting for you here. Come back tomorrow evening "

But I was not reassured. I remembered the fox. One runs the risk of weeping a little, if one lets himself be tamed...

26.

Beside the well there was the ruin of an old stone wall. When I came back from my work, the next evening, I saw from some distance away my little prince sitting on top of this wall, with his feet dangling. And I heard him say :

"Then you don't remember. This is not the exact spot."

Another voice must have answered him, for he replied to it :

"Yes, yes ! It is the right day, but this is not the place."

I continued my walk toward the wall. At no time did I see or hear anyone. The little prince, however, replied once again :

"—Exactly. You will see where my track begins, in the sand. You have nothing to do but wait for me there. I shall be there tonight."

I was only twenty yards from the wall, and I still saw nothing.

After a silence the little prince spoke again :

" You have good poison? You are sure that it will not make me suffer too long ? "

I stopped in my tracks, my heart torn asunder ; but still I did not understand.

" Now go away," said the little prince. " I want to get down from the wall."

I dropped my eyes, then, to the foot of the wall—and I leaped

"Now go away . . . I want to get down from the wall."

into the air. There before me, facing the little prince, was one of those yellow snakes that take thirty seconds to bring your life to an end. Even as I was digging into my pocket to get out my revolver I made a running step back. But, at the noise I made, the snake let himself flow easily across the sand like the dying spray of a fountain, and, in no apparent hurry, disappeared, with a light metallic sound, among the stones.

I reached the wall just in time to catch my little man in my arms ; his face was white as snow.

" What does this mean ?" I demanded. " Why are you talking with snakes ?"

I had loosened the golden muffler that he always wore. I had moistened his temples, and had given him some water to drink. And now I did not dare ask him any more questions. He looked at me very gravely, and put his arms around my neck. I felt his heart beating like the heart of a dying bird, shot with someone's rifle...

" I am glad that you have found what was the matter with your engine," he said. " Now you can go back home—"

" How do you know about that ?"

I was just coming to tell him that my work had been successful, beyond anything that I had dared to hope.

He made no answer to my question, but he added :

" I, too, am going back home today ..."

Then, sadly—

" It is much farther ... It is much more difficult ..."

I realized clearly that something extraordinary was happening. I was holding him close in my arms as if he were a little child ; and yet it seemed to me that he was rushing headlong toward an abyss from which I could do nothing to restrain him ...

His look was very serious, like some one lost far away.

" I have your sheep. And I have the sheep's box. And I have the muzzle ..."

And he gave me a sad smile.

I waited a long time. I could see that he was reviving little by little.

" Dear little man," I said to him, " You are afraid ..."

He was afraid, there was no doubt about that. But he laughed lightly.

" I shall be much more afraid this evening ..."

Once again I felt myself frozen by the sense of something irreparable. And I knew that I could not bear the thought of never hearing that laughter any more. For me, it was like a spring of fresh water in the desert.

" Little man," I said, " I want to hear you laugh again."

But he said to me :

" Tonight, it will be a year ... My star, then, can be found right above the place where I came to the Earth, a year ago ..."

" Little man," I said, " tell me that it is only a bad dream—this affair of the snake, and the meeting-place, and the star ..."

But he did not answer my plea. He said to me, instead :

" The thing that is important is the thing that is not seen ..."

" Yes, I know ..."

" It is just as it is with the flower. If you love a flower that lives on a star, it is sweet to look at the sky at night. All the stars are a-bloom with flowers ... "

" Yes, I know ..."

" It is just as it is with the water. Because of the pulley, and the rope, what you gave me to drink was like music. You remember—how good it was."

" Yes, I know ..."

" And at night you will look up at the stars. Where I live everything is so small that I cannot show you where my star is to be found. It is better, like that. My star will be just one of the stars, for you. And so you will love to watch all the stars in the heavens ... They will all be your friends. And, besides, I am going to make you a present..."

He laughed again.

" Ah, little prince, dear little prince ! I love to hear that laughter !"

" That is my present. Just that. I will be as it was when we drank the water ..."

" What are you trying to say ?"

" All men have stars," he answered, " but they are not the same things for different people. For some, who are travelers, the stars are guides. For others they are no more than little lights in the sky. For others, who are scholars, they are problems. For my businessman they are wealth. But all these stars are silent. You—you alone—will have the stars as no one else has them—"

" What are you trying to say ?"

" In one of the stars I shall be living. In one of them I shall be laughing. And so it will be as if all the stars were laughing, when you look at the sky at night ... You—only you—will have stars that can laugh !"

And he laughed again.

" And when your sorrow is comforted (time soothes all sorrows) you will be content that you have known me. You will always be my friend. You will want to laugh with me. And you will sometimes open your window, so, for that pleasure ... And your friends will be properly astonished to see you laughing as you look up at the sky ! Then you will say to them, ' Yes, the stars always make me laugh !' And they will think you are crazy. It will be a very shabby trick that I shall have played on you ..."

And he laughed again.

" It will be as if, in place of the stars, I had given you a great number of little bells that knew how to laugh ..."

And he laughed again. Then he quickly became serious :

" Tonight—you know ... Do not come."

" I shall not leave you," I said.

" I shall look as if I were suffering. I shall look a little as if I were dying. It is like that. Do not come to see that. It is not worth the trouble ..."

" I shall not leave you."

But he was worried.

" I tell you—it is also because of the snake. He must not bite you. Snakes—they are malicious creatures. This one might bite you just for fun ..."

" I shall not leave you."

But a thought came to reassure him :

" It is true that they have no more poison for a second bite."

That night I did not see him set out on his way. He got away from me without making a sound. When I succeeded in catching up with him he was walking along with a quick and resolute step. He said to me merely :

" Ah ! You are there ..."

And he took me by the hand. But he was still worrying.

" It was wrong of you to come. You will suffer. I shall look as if I were dead ; and that will not be true ..."

I said nothing.

" You understand ... It is too far. I cannot carry this body with me. It is too heavy."

I said nothing.

" But it will be like an old abandoned shell. There is nothing sad about old shells..."

I said nothing.

He was a little discouraged. But he made one more effort :

" You know, it will be very nice. I, too, shall look at the stars. All the stars will be wells with a rusty pulley. All the stars will pour out fresh water for me to drink ..."

I said nothing.

" That will be so amusing ! You will have five hundred million little bells, and I shall have five hundred million springs of fresh water ..."

And he too said nothing more, because he was crying ...

" Here it is. Let me go on by myself."

And he sat down, because he was so afraid. Then he said, again :

" You know—my flower ... I am responsible for her. And she is so weak ! She is so naïve! She has four thorns, of no use at all, to protect herself against all the world ..."

I too sat down, because I was not able to stand up any longer.

" There now—that is all ..."

He still hesitated a little ; then he got up. He took one step. I could not move.

There was nothing there but a flash of yellow close to his ankle. He remained motionless for an instant. He did not cry out. He fell as gently as a tree falls. There was not even any sound, because of the sand.

"He fell as gently as a tree falls. There was not ever any sound . . ."

27

And now six years have already gone by ... I have never yet told this story. The companions who met me on my return were well content to see me alive. I was sad, but I told them : " I am tired."

Now my sorrow is comforted a little. That is to say—not entirely. But I know that he did go back to his planet, because I did not find his body at daybreak. It was not such a heavy body ... And at night I love to listen to the stars. It is like five hundred million little bells ...

But there is one extraordinary thing ... When I drew the muzzle for the little prince, I forgot to add the leather strap to it. He will never have been able to fasten it on his sheep. So now I keep wondering : what is happening on his planet ? Perhaps the sheep has eaten the flower ...

At one time I say to myself : " Surely not ! The little prince shuts his flower under her glass globe every night, and he watches over his sheep very carefully ..." Then I am happy. And there is sweetness in the laughter of all the stars.

But at another time I say to myself : " At some moment or other one is absent-minded, and that is enough ! On some one evening he forgot the glass globe, or the sheep got out, without making any noise, in the night ..." And then the little bells are changed to tears ...

Here, then, is a great mystery. For you who also love the little prince, and for me, nothing in the universe can be the same if somewhere, we do not know where, a sheep that we never saw has—yes or no ? —eaten a rose ...

Look up at the sky. Ask yourselves : Is it yes or no ? Has the sheep eaten the flower ? And you will see how everything changes ...

And no grown-up will ever understand that this is a matter of so much importance!

This is, to me, the loveliest and saddest landscape in the world. It is the same as that on page 183, but I have drawn it again to impress it on your memory. It is here that the little prince appeared on Earth, and disappeared.

Look at it carefully so that you will be sure to recognize it in case you travel some day to the African desert. And, if you should come upon this spot, please do not hurry on. Wait for a time, exactly under the star. Then, if a little man appears who laughs, who has golden hair and who refuses to answer questions, you will know who he is. If this should happen, please comfort me. Send me word that he has come back.

國家圖書館出版品預行編目資料

小王子／聖‧修伯里／著　楊玉娘／譯
-- 修訂一版-- 新北市：新潮社，2018.06
面；　公分
ISBN　978-986-316-706-8　（平裝）

876.57　　　　　　　　　　　　107005552

小王子

聖‧修伯里／著

楊玉娘／譯

【策　劃】林郁
【出版人】翁天培
【製　作】天蠍座文創
【出　版】新潮社文化事業有限公司
電話：(02) 8666-5711
傳真：(02) 8666-5833
E-mail：service@xcsbook.com.tw

【總經銷】創智文化有限公司
新北市土城區忠承路89號6F（永寧科技園區）
電話：(02) 2268-3489
傳真：(02) 2269-6560

印前作業　東豪印刷事業有限公司

修訂一版　2018年06月
一版六刷　2022年05月